Alex and the Raynhams

Iris Bromige

CORONET BOOKS
Hodder Paperbacks Ltd., London

Copyright © 1961 by Iris Bromige
First published in Great Britain by
Hodder & Stoughton Ltd., 1961
Coronet edition 1972
Second impression 1973

The characters and situations in this book are entirely imaginary and bear no relation to any real person or actual happening.

This book is sold subject to the condition that it shall not, by way of trade or otherwise, be lent, re-sold, hired out or otherwise circulated without the publisher's prior consent in any form of binding or cover other than that in which this is published and without a similar condition including this condition being imposed on the subsequent purchaser.

Printed and bound in Great Britain for
Coronet Books, Hodder Paperbacks Ltd,
St. Paul's House, Warwick Lane,
London, EC4P 4AH
by Hunt Barnard Printing Ltd,
Aylesbury, Bucks.

ISBN 0 340 15953 7

Chapter One

"AND what is the pretty bridesmaid doing here, hidden away all on her own?"

Alexandra Madison looked up, startled, and put her cup of tea on the floor as she uncurled herself from the sofa.

"Now don't let me disturb you. I've only come to see if I left my fur stole here. I had it when your brother brought me in here to see that exquisite little ivory carving which was your grandmother's."

"I don't think it's here, Mrs . . ." Alex hesitated, searching for the name.

"Raynham. Ian's godmother."

"I'm sorry. I should have known, but there were so many people at the wedding."

"Yes. A perfectly beautiful wedding. Such a lovely bride, and dear Ian so charming. I adore weddings, don't you? Now don't worry about the stole. I must have left it in the hall. I'm dreadfully careless. Just go on with your tea and tell me why you were looking so pensive. You should be with the party, bewitching the young men."

Alex, normally not attracted by such gushing charm, found herself yielding to the dazzling, sympathetic smile which Mrs Raynham bent on her as she sat down beside her.

"Well, I really came in here to see how our dog was. He's very old, and nearly blind, so we thought we'd better shut him up here in the study. He gets miserable, though, if he's left alone too long, so I thought I'd just come in here for a quiet cup of tea and keep him company. Now he's gone to sleep again. He sleeps an awful lot."

Mrs Raynham bent to stroke the head of the golden retriever curled up on the rug as she said,

"Poor dear. It's so sad when they grow old. We have an old dog, too. A spaniel. But let's not talk of old age on a wedding day. You were looking a little sad. You'll miss Rosalind, I expect. You and she ran a book shop together, I believe."

"Yes. At least, Rosalind managed it, and I was a not terribly good assistant. I liked reading the books too much. Dipping in. Spent far too much time in the stock room. Somehow, I can't go through a pile of books without opening one or two."

"And now you're left alone to cope?"

"Oh no, we've sold the business. I didn't want to run it on my own. Now I'm trying to find the kind of job I'd really like, but it's awfully difficult."

"Tell me what you'd really like," said Mrs Raynham, smiling as she leaned back and regarded Alex as though she found her the most interesting person in the world.

"Well, I love the country and animals and birds, and I wouldn't like to be cooped up in an office all day. And . . ."

"Go on."

"I like writing. About animals and the country. I've sent one or two articles to our local paper and had one published."

"Well, now, this really is exciting. I do believe providence intended us to meet. I'm looking for a resident secretary. I live in the country. I'm a journalist, free lance, and I help to edit a country magazine called *Downland Journal*. Perhaps you've heard of it. No, probably not. It only has a local sale, and although we're not far away, I don't suppose it's reached here."

"No, I haven't come across it," said Alex, a little bewildered, for Mrs Raynham, exquisitely dressed, charmingly sophisticated, seemed as far removed from country matters as a diamond necklace from a mine.

"There wouldn't be an awful lot for you to do, and you would have plenty of freedom. Although we live within easy reach of London, the country is really very lovely. Bridgefield. Do you know it?"

"Yes. At least, I've cycled over that stretch of the North Downs. But I'm not a very good typist, and I haven't done any shorthand since I went to a short business course after I left school. I never wanted to go into an office, but Daddy thought that a little business training would come in useful, anyway. I believe he hoped I'd deal with the business side of the family timber estate."

"I know. Cheap labour," said Mrs Raynham gaily. "You come along and work with me. I'm sure we'd get along splendidly. I have a nice family, and you'll be near enough to come home for week-ends whenever you want to. I'd pay you seven guineas a week, all found, as they say, and give you a little guidance with your country articles, and an introduction to David Barling, my editor. What do you say?"

"But . . . I don't know . . . It's a bit sudden."

"All the best things in life happen like that," declared Mrs Raynham. "Falling in love, making friends. I don't believe in caution. Meet life eagerly, with open hands. That's my philosophy." She had a beautiful voice and she declaimed like an actress, so that Alex found herself almost hypnotised. She was fumbling for an answer when the door opened and her brother came in, looking annoyed.

"Alex, have you gone to ground again?" He turned to Mrs Raynham with a polite smile. "Excuse me, Mrs Raynham, but I seem to have spent half my life chasing after my sister and bringing her back to her social duties. She has an awful habit of vanishing from parties and doesn't seem to realise that it's discourteous."

"Then we're both at fault, dear boy," said Mrs Raynham, turning the dazzle on to him. "She looked so pensive, poor sweet, when I came in here and found her all alone that I just had to find out more about her, and we've had the most interesting conversation, and I've found a delightful secretary into the bargain."

It was Clive's turn to look bewildered, and Alex's eyes sparkled mischievously.

"Mrs Raynham has offered me a job," she said slowly and sweetly, as though to a rather obtuse child.

"But you've had no training or experience as a secretary."

"Isn't that just like a brother?" Mrs Raynham's tinkling laugh danced round the book-lined study.

"Are you serious about this, Mrs Raynham?"

The blue eyes opened wide as she looked up at his dark face.

"But of course, dear boy. Ah, you think I'm a silly, irrational woman to engage somebody I've only just met, but I believe in feminine intuition. I know Alex is just the person I'm looking for. Our wavelengths are sympathetic. A lovely bridesmaid. A charming secretary. When could you start, my dear?"

"I'll have to work it out . . ."

"Of course. Now it's only ten days to Christmas, and I'm madly busy with shopping and planning parties. My present secretary has promised to stay one more week although, poor sweet, she's up to her eyes in moving. Married two years and only just found a house. So sad for them, living in dreary rooms all this time. Shall we say the first of January? We'll start the New Year together."

"But . . ."

"Now I simply mustn't keep you away from the party any longer or your brother will be really cross with me. Here's my card, dear. Come along and see me next Saturday morning. That's the only day I shall be free next week. Then I can show you the house, introduce you to the children, if they're home, and we can discuss the whole project in detail."

"What time?" asked Alex.

"About eleven, dear. I shall look forward to seeing your bright face again. Such beautiful red hair. Unusual to have that lovely colour with such a silky texture. So often it's coarse, like grass stalks. And blue-green eyes, the colour of tropical seas. Quite enchanting. I think," she added, regarding Alex dreamily with her head on one side, much to the girl's embarrassment, "yes, I think I'd have chosen a duck-egg blue rather than that forget-me-not shade for your dress. Not that you don't look positively enchanting. But duck-egg is ravishing with your colouring. Now I simply must go and find my stole. Lucky young man to have such a charming sister," she concluded, patting Clive's arm as she passed him, and pausing at the door to smile back at Alex, as though well aware of the attractive picture she made in the doorway in her beautifully cut grey silk suit with a diamond brooch winking in the lapel, and many rows of pearls round her slender neck. Her hair was pale gold and her make-up so perfect that it was difficult to guess her age. She had the tall, slim figure of a girl, but her superb poise and assurance belonged to maturity, and her eyes, too, suggested that her youth had been left gracefully behind. Alex guessed her to be in her forties. In fact, Barbara Raynham was fifty-three.

"Well!" exclaimed Clive, as the door closed behind her and he sat down on the arm of the sofa as though bereft of strength. "What an act! Are you crazy, Alex, to get mixed up with that silly woman?"

"It sounds a pleasant job, and much more interesting than any I've seen so far."

"If you're going to do secretarial work, you might as well stay at home and help Dad. You've always been so happy here."

"I know. But things have changed, and I want to get away, Clive."

He looked at her as she stood up, shaking out her frilly skirt. That woman was right, he thought. Alex had grown from a gawky, bizarre girl into a very attractive young woman.

"How have they changed? I know you'll miss Rosalind, and the business has been sold, but you didn't want to keep it going."

"It's not that, but somehow, here at Camerino, things have been pared away from me over the last years."

"Things, or people? Go on, get it off your chest. I've thought for some time that you weren't so contented here as you used to be. Let's have it."

"Well, it's been a gradual process, I suppose. First I lost Sarah to you."

"My dear, you gained a sister-in-law."

"And lost a friend. No, that's not fair to Sarah."

"You're dead right. It's not. She's still as fond of you as ever she was."

"Yes, but you don't share people, Clive. You two are wrapped up in each other and the children. It's natural. I'm not complaining. I knew it was inevitable, but that doesn't mean that I haven't missed Sarah. And you, too, for that matter."

"But we're only a short walk away, and you know how welcome you always are."

"I know. But it's not the same. Then Delia's stayed in Switzerland all these years, and I don't expect she'll ever come to live here again."

"She likes running her hotel too much. Since Aunt Isobel left it to her, it's become the most important thing in her life. I'm sorry, too, that we see so little of her."

"Now Rosalind's married. And Grandma . . ." Alex's bottom lip quivered and she stooped to poke up the dying embers of the fire.

Clive's eyes were kind as he looked at his sister. The death of old Mrs Madison a year ago had been a sad blow to all of them, but on Alex it had perhaps fallen most heavily, for there had been a special bond between the old lady and her youngest grandchild.

"She was eighty-four, Alex. It was perhaps kinder for her to go before her mind lost its clarity and her senses failed. She felt that she had lived long enough when the time came, you know."

"Yes. That doesn't make it any easier for us, though. It seems so strange, not having her there in the garden wing. To have it closed and empty. I feel that bit by bit my life's been impoverished. I want to get away, Clive. When we waved Rosalind off just now, I felt as though the last bit of the old life had gone from me."

"Yes, I can see your point. Perhaps it would be better for you to spread your wings now, but not in this hare-brained fashion, my dear. You're so impetuous. Such a step needs care and planning. We could have a family conference."

"Live dangerously. That's Mrs Raynham's philosophy. I must say she looks pretty happy on it."

"She's well armed and able to take care of herself. You're young and inexperienced."

"Then it's time I got some experience. I've made up my mind. I shall accept her offer."

"Alex! You know absolutely nothing about this woman, or the work you'll have to do, or the home you'll be taken into. For heaven's sake be practical. Find out more about the job before you commit yourself, or, better still, take more time to look around. Rosalind has barely left on her honeymoon, and here you are deciding that you must fly off at once."

She smiled at him a little unhappily.

"I know. Headstrong brat. But this has been boiling up for a long time, Clive. And I'm not a planner. I prefer to take a chance. Live dangerously," she added mischievously, knowing how strongly her rational brother would disapprove of such philosophy.

"Well, this isn't the time to discuss it. We'd better get back to the reception, and we'll talk about it again. I'll see if I can find out more about Mrs Raynham from Ian's mother."

"I do think everything's an anti-climax after the bride has gone. I think the festivities should be brought to a close then."

"Well, most of the fringe have gone. We're only left with the inner core, so come along and help pass the cups of tea round."

Alex stooped to pat Bruno and then followed her brother out. No matter what Clive found out, she thought, she would accept this post Mrs Raynham offered her. Camerino had become too full of ghosts for her. She had to stop mourning for them and find something to take their place. At twenty-five, she was surely old enough to look after herself. Anyone would think to hear Clive talk that she was still in her teens.

As she helped to pass round more cups of tea to the remaining guests, most of whom hovered round the display of presents, nobody would have guessed from her smiling face and gay manner that she felt as forlorn as a ship's cat on a deserted vessel. Out of the corner of her eye, she saw Clive talking to the bridegroom's mother, but Mrs Raynham had gone. It's no use, my boy, thought Alex. My mind's made up. When, a few minutes later, she saw him cross the room to join his wife, he was frowning. She watched him talking to Sarah, and saw Sarah lay a hand on his arm, half smiling. Sarah would back her up, she thought. She could always rely on Sarah's sympathy and understanding, even though she was now so firmly possessed by Clive and their son and the new baby who was Alex's god-daughter. She wondered what Sarah was saying as their eyes met across the room and Sarah gave her a reassuring little wave.

"Impulsiveness can sometimes bring its own rewards, Clive. I think you're unduly worried about it. After all, she won't be far away. It's not as though she's contemplating going abroad," said Sarah.

"Well, we can be sure that if she's set her mind on it, we shan't deflect her."

"She's a Madison, dear," said his wife demurely.

"She's the image of the old lady," said Clive.

"She misses her dreadfully, you know. I think this sort of job, where she'll be living with a family, will be the right thing for her just now. She's a warm-hearted girl, and she needs companionship."

"Depends on the family, doesn't it?"

"She'll soon find out whether she likes them or not. Alex is nothing if not decisive in making up her mind about people. She can easily give it up if she's not happy there. Don't fuss, darling. Alex has a charmed life. She's always pitched headlong into things, and she's always come up smiling."

"There's usually been someone to help fish her out."

"She fishes herself out remarkably well, too. But she's not happy now, Clive. I've been worried at the way she looks these days if you catch her unawares. An odd, quenched look. She's lonely and unhappy. I think any venture, even if it turns out to be a disappointment, is preferable to this blankness in her life. I shall keep in touch with her, you can be sure."

"Well, between you, of course, I don't stand a chance," said Clive, putting an arm round his wife's shoulder. "Mother and Dad will feel it, though."

"They'll know it's time Alex made her own life. What an

attractive young woman she's grown into! Beats the lot, you know, Clive."

"When she bothers to dress properly and take a little trouble."

"You can't overlook her, anyway," said Sarah, laughing. "I wonder if there are any susceptible young men in Mrs Raynham's circle."

"Well, a squib is being thrown into their midst. If they like a nice quiet, peaceful life, I'm sorry for them, although, judging by Mrs Raynham, they'll probably be a family of gadabout half-wits, anyway."

"Now stop being a Jonah and come and say some soothing words to Alex. She's got the glint of battle in her eyes. Let's disarm her by drinking a toast to her new venture."

"I've drunk enough toasts to-day, but I dare say I could manage a few kind words."

And thus it was that Alex won her victory far more easily than she had expected, and made of her sister's wedding day a day of importance in her own life, too.

Chapter Two

WHEN Alex arrived at Bridgefield Station, she asked the porter if he could direct her to Pelham House, and after scratching his head for a moment, he said,

"What road?"

"I don't know. All it says on this card is Pelham House, Bridgefield."

"Just swank, not putting in the road. Wait a sec. I'll ask my chum."

A conference with his chum in the booking-office elicited the information that Pelham House was half way down a lane just beyond the church and that it was a good twenty minutes' walk. Alex thanked them, glanced at her watch, and set off briskly, wishing that she had been able to borrow her father's car. Bridgefield, once a pretty little village and now verging on a town to meet the demands of an ever-growing population, had changed a lot since Alex had last seen it, but it was still surrounded by common land and looked clean and pleasant on that mild, bright December morning. Pelham House was set well back from the lane behind a high brick wall, and as Alex went through the wrought-iron gates, she found herself outside a pretty little lodge with leaded-light windows and mellow red bricks. There was no sign of life, however, and she walked on up the semi-circular drive towards the large white house with green shutters which was half hidden by a group of birch trees on the front lawn. As she approached the green door between two white columns, it opened and Mrs Raynham stood there and welcomed her with outstretched arms and a radiant smile.

"And here's my charming secretary. I should have had you met at the station, dear, but Bruce, the bad lad, borrowed my car and although he promised faithfully to be back by half-past ten, he still hasn't arrived. Do you drive, dear? It would be so useful if you do."

"Yes."

"Splendid. What did I say? I knew I'd hit on a treasure. I don't like driving myself. It will be such an advantage to have you able to act as chauffeuse. Now come along in, dear, and have a glass of sherry with me before I show you round."

Half way through their glass of sherry, the drawing-room door opened to admit a tall, fair young man who came up to his mother holding up his hands in mock terror like a prisoner facing a gun, but he was smiling as he said,

"Shoot, darling. I met a friend, and he asked me in for a drink. You know how it is, and after all, it's practically Christmas."

"You're a naughty boy, Bruce, and it's to Miss Madison, here, that you should apologise."

He fell on his knee before Alex and put his hand on his heart.

"If I'd known what I was missing, no friend would have

kept me from the station. I'm delighted to know you, Miss Madison. Congratulations, Mother. May I join the sherry party?"

"Well, we'll have to forgive you, I suppose. Pour me another, darling. Alex?"

"No thank you."

"Alex? Short for Alexandra?" asked Bruce, pouring the drinks.

"Yes."

"It suits you. I'm sure we're going to enjoy having you here, Alex. You'll brighten up the landscape no end."

"We shall all love having her," declared his mother, and it occurred to Alex that nobody would think she was coming here to work.

"I hope I'll be able to do the work satisfactorily, Mrs Raynhim. I've had no secretarial experience, you know."

"Mother's chatty little columns won't tax you, Alex. Our Dorinda knows her stuff. All you have to do is copy her atrocious hand-writing."

"I never have been able to compose on to a machine. I always have to write it. Dorinda is the name I write under for a monthly fashion column I do for one of the glossies. I always used that name when I was a full-time journalist in London. I use my own name for our *Downland Journal*. More suitable for that type of publication."

"Do you write on fashion for that, then?" asked Alex, a little bewildered.

"Not exactly, but I write on all subjects that interest women. David, that's the editor, used to run it on his own, solely on country topics. It had a wretched little sale, and I told him that he was on the wrong track, or, at least, running on only one track instead of two." Barbara Raynham put her glass down and leaned back in the chair, obviously in her element. "Bridgefield, I said, is no longer a tiny rural community. It's an outpost of London. More Bridgefield men work in London now than ever work locally as craftsmen or farmers or what have you. Their wives go up to London for theatres and shopping. This is a community with one foot in the country and one in London. You must cater for it accordingly. He was a little stubborn, but I won him over."

"Who could resist your magnetism, darling? Not the worthy, stolid David Barling. Nothing like you had ever hit him before," said Bruce, grinning.

"You should take my professional ability more seriously, dear."

"But I do, darling. You know your job. Salesmanship is part of it, and my, you're some saleswoman!"

"Well, David is a little amateurish, let's admit it. A fine, dependable person, but a teeny weeny bit old-fashioned. *Strand Magazine* era. He didn't seem to realise that it is women who are the chief buyers of magazines, and that if he let me cater for their interests alongside his country interests, we'd be catering for the whole population of Bridgefield instead of a few bird watchers and fishermen. In the end I overcame his scruples, though it was a hard fight. But I mustn't run on." She turned a dazzling smile on Alex again. "Time enough for you to find out all about that. Now come along and see the room I've chosen for you. I want you to be completely comfortable and happy with us, Alex dear."

The house was gaily and beautifully furnished, and Mrs Raynham's own personality was reflected in all the rooms except her husband's study, which was austere and rather gloomy, a fact which Mrs. Raynham commented on as she closed the door after their peep inside.

"Dreadfully dreary, but dear Leonard likes it just as it is, and as he is the only person who ever goes in there, we can humour him."

The room allotted to Alex was a large room on the first floor, furnished as a bed-sitting room, with the gay colours and sumptuous curtains which characterised the whole house.

"We look forward to your living with us as one of the family, dear, but you may like to be on your own sometimes, so we turned this into a bed-sitting room."

"I think it's very nice indeed, Mrs Raynham. I'm sure I shall be comfortable here. Of course, I shall probably go home quite often at the week-ends."

"Whenever you wish, Alex. I shouldn't dream of stealing you away from your family. Now there's just my study to show you and your own office, which leads out of it."

By the time Alex returned to the drawing-room, she had decided that this job offered everything she could wish for. Already her spirits had responded to the gay atmosphere of the household, and the feeling of blank inertia which was so foreign to her nature and which had dogged her for weeks past, had vanished. In the drawing-room, a pretty, fair girl was hugging the fire. She smiled as she turned, and the likeness to Mrs Raynham was startling.

"Ah, Juliet, I'm glad you're here to meet my new secretary before she goes. Miss Madison. No, I think we should make it Alex from the start, don't you? Alex, this is my youngest child, Juliet."

Mrs Raynham's looks and charm plus youth were almost more than any girl had a right to, thought Alex, as she expressed her pleasure at meeting Juliet.

"Mother, do you know if . . .?" The speaker at the open door stopped and hesitated, then said hurriedly; "Oh, I'm sorry, I thought you were alone."

"Well, don't stand there like an unwanted waif, dear. Come in and meet my new secretary. This is my other daughter, Beth, Alex, who is the mainstay of the home. She's so wonderful at running this house and relieving me of all the little domestic worries that I always maintain that what little success I have had as a journalist is due to Beth."

Beth, who looked a good deal older than her brother and sister, broke the pattern of fair good looks, for she was dark, with a sallow skin and insignificant features. Alex guessed that she was shy, although she looked composed as she greeted her with a tentative, rather sweet smile. She wore horn-rimmed glasses which were too heavy for her small face.

"Now you've met all the family," said Mrs Raynham.

"What about Nigel? Fancy not counting him, and he thinks he's so important," said Juliet mischievously.

"Of course I count him, but he's not a Raynham. Nigel is my son by my first marriage, Alex. I married when I was a mere child, just eighteen, and I was only twenty when Nigel was born. Far too young to marry, but we were divinely happy. Poor Richard was killed in an aeroplane crash only a few months after Nigel was born. So Nigel is only partly connected with us, if you see what I mean."

"And the slighter the connection the better, as far as he is concerned," said Juliet.

"Now darling, don't be naughty. We all get on splendidly, just because we all respect each other's personalities. And in any case, you can't say Nigel bothers us much. I'd like to see more of him. Now that he's taken the lodge for the summer, I hope we shall."

"Oh, Nigel's all right. Just infuriating," said Juliet, smiling.

"I've a brother like that," said Alex.

"Not like Nigel. There couldn't be two Nigels, but don't be alarmed. He keeps his distance and only casts a mocking smile in our direction now and again."

"Who?" asked Bruce, coming in, rubbing his hands.

"Nigel."

"His lordship's all right. Knows what he wants, and has made a nice comfortable life for himself, if you ask me."

"Mother, is Father coming home to lunch today?" asked Beth, hovering by the door again, as though urgent business in the kitchen awaited her.

"Father? No, darling. He's much too busy. He telephoned an hour ago. I'm so sorry. I forgot to tell you. In the excitement of having Alex here, it went out of my mind."

"No wonder," said Bruce with an impudent smile at Alex.

"Now you can drive Alex to the station, Bruce dear, can't you? She wants to catch the twelve-thirty train."

"It will be a privilege and a pleasure."

Juliet joined her mother at the door to wave them off, and Alex was so touched by their warm friendliness that she said to Bruce as the car moved slowly down the drive,

"What a delightful family you have! I really am looking forward to taking up this job."

"We're looking forward to having you. The last secretary mother had was a sweet girl, but terribly serious-minded. She left yesterday. She was married and didn't live in. Mother prefers to have a resident secretary, though. Her work's a bit spasmodic and doesn't fit into regular hours very well. Mother's rather a spasmodic sort of person, bless her. I'm sure you'll enjoy working for her, though."

"I know I shall."

He lifted his arm in a salute as a black Jaguar passed them. Alex caught a glimpse of a rather languid, yellow-gloved hand returning the salute.

"That was Nigel," said Bruce.

"Oh. Why does he live in the lodge?"

"He's only just taken it. He had a bachelor flat in London. He's a bio-chemist. One of the test-tube boys. Rather a bright one, too. His firm have recently bought an old manor house on the other side of Elton and converted it into a Research Station. A bit too inconveniently placed for travelling between there and London every day, so his nibs gave up his flat, and bought a plot of land not far from the Research Station, where he's going to build his ideal home. We're close enough to his job and the plot of land to be a convenient base for him while his house is going up. He finds family life impossible, but the lodge is sufficiently detached to be bearable, and he's brought his man, Ben, to look after him."

"He sounds an eccentric sort of person, your half-brother."

"Not really. Just knows what he wants and gets it. I admire him in a way, though sometimes I'd like to shoot him. Here we are. All too short." He glanced at his watch. "Ten minutes to wait. Good."

"Please don't bother," said Alex, as he slid out of the car to join her.

"Haven't you grasped yet that I find your company highly agreeable, Alex?" he asked, grinning. "I can't believe you're slow on the uptake."

Her blue-green eyes surveyed him gravely. Her experience of young men was in fact extremely limited, for she had led a quiet, sheltered life and had never been much attracted by the opposite sex, considering them more often than not a fatuous nuisance. The laughing blue eyes of this young man, however, had a peculiarly melting effect on her. Her head was spinning, too, from the effect of the combined Raynham charm. She was not used to having compliments showered on her like confetti, for her own family was given to plain speaking and no nonsense.

"We hardly know each other," she said simply.

"All the more reason to waste no time. How old are you, Alex?"

"Twenty-five."

"You look younger. No attachments?"

"What sort?"

"Young men, of course."

"No."

"Good heavens, are all the males blind in your circle?"

"I haven't met many. I've other interests."

He threw back his head and laughed.

"Impossible! But tell me what they are."

"Country life. Birds and animals. I like walking in the country better than anything."

"Alone?"

"Usually."

"For crying out loud! Haven't you ever wanted companions of your own age?"

"Not until lately. I had my sisters and brother when I was younger. But they've all left home now, and that's why I decided to find a new job. My old life has closed up, somehow."

"If you ask me, it's high time you came out of hiding. You've enough vitality in your face to power a jet plane, and you've been living in a burrow like a little rabbit, depriving the world."

"I don't know how to handle so many compliments," said Alex, her cheeks dimpling.

"Here." He grabbed her and pulled her into the doorway of a small brick structure on the platform. Two porters sat inside brewing tea. "No objection, boys?" called Bruce over his shoulder, pointing to the sprig of mistletoe stuck over the doorway. They grinned as Bruce kissed Alex with enthusiasm, and then they all wished each other a Happy Christmas as the train came in.

"It's the New Year I'm looking forward to," said Bruce, as he opened a carriage door for her.

"Me, too," said Alex, smiling at him, unable to resist his infectious charm, although if anybody had told her she would enjoy such foolish impudence, she would have denied it with scorn.

When she arrived home and told her parents all about it, her enthusiasm was so unbounded that they felt reassured. Only Clive, that evening, struck a cautionary note.

"No family is as perfect as that. For heaven's sake don't go pouring yourself out in your usual all or nothing way until you've been there for a month or two."

"Poor old Clive. Always the pessimist. Be a dear, and help me hang up these lanterns."

He looked at her as she stood on the ladder, two paper lanterns in one hand, a length of twine in the other, her hair gleaming like copper in firelight, her slender legs a picture which even her brother could appreciate. He sighed. What could you say to innocence? She was warm-hearted and honest herself, and she accepted everybody at their face value. She often took dislikes to people, but always for silly reasons, in his opinion. She disliked stuffy people, and was not interested in what might lie beneath the stuffiness. She was impatient with ponderous or pretentious people, and she had once refused to remain in the house while a medical scientist who admitted to using animals for experiments was under their roof, and she had found it hard to forgive her father for knowing such a monster. She did nothing by halves. She loved with all her heart, loyally and generously, and she disliked with considerable fervour, too. She seemed to him to be without the right kind of armour to meet the world, but then he supposed youth usually was. Alex was only starting out at a later date than most young people.

"What do you want me to do?" he asked, resignedly.

"Tell me if they're straight, and then hand me the scissors."

He supposed he was fussing unnecessarily, as Sarah had said.

These Raynhams sounded very pleasant people, and Ian's mother had been fairly reassuring. He was suspicious of so much charm, but it could be the reflection of genuine good nature.

"You didn't see Mr Raynham, did you?" he asked.

"No. He's a very busy man, I gathered. I don't believe they see much of him. Immersed in business. I don't know what his business is."

"He owns a chain of hardware shops, among other things. Built them up from one little shop in the suburbs, and has only taken ten years to do it. He's getting into property development now, I believe. A formidable type, I'd say."

"How do you know all this?"

"I get around," said Clive, grinning.

"No wonder they don't see much of him at home, then. He must be nice to have such a delightful family, though. What's bred in the bone, as Grandma used to say."

"Sarah wants to know if you'll come round tomorrow and help her decorate the Christmas tree. Come to dinner."

"Goody. I'd love to. I adore Christmas trees."

"You really are walking on air now that you've landed this job, aren't you?"

She sat on the top step of the ladder, scissors and twine in her hands, and beamed down at him.

"Yes. It's going to be a wonderful New Year for me. I feel it in my bones. And by next Christmas, I may be an established journalist myself. Who knows?"

"With Mrs Raynham your fairy godmother, and Pelham House the land of smiles. Well, well. Who knows? I must go. Whenever I just look in to say good evening to the parents, I get collared for about half a dozen little jobs."

"Sarah won't shout at you for being late for dinner. She's much too submissive," said Alex mischievously.

"Don't know why I worry about what's going to happen to you at the Raynhams'. I should be feeling sorry for them. So long, sister."

"See you tomorrow, man of sorrow," said Alex.

Chapter Three

BY the end of her first week at Pelham House, Alex had confirmed that her optimism was justified, for she was completely happy in her new occupation, which offered her variety, companionship, bright surroundings and a carefree atmosphere. She spent most of the morning in her office at the typewriter, dealing with her employer's private correspondence, which was considerable, and articles on interior decorating and flower arrangements for the *Downland Journal*. The latter she typed from Mrs Raynham's manuscript, but the letters were dictated, with many irreverent and witty asides which kept Alex bubbling with laughter. Nobody remotely like Barbara Raynham had ever come Alex's way before, and she was bewitched by her scintillating charm. When her employer left the house, as she did on most days as soon as the office work was finished, the air felt appreciably flatter, like boiled water after champagne, but perhaps a diet of nothing but champagne would be too much of a good thing, thought Alex on the Friday morning as she watched Mrs Raynham run out to the drive where Bruce was waiting to drive her to the station to catch the fast train to London. That week she had been making tours of the West End sales for her fashion column, but Alex had learned from Bruce that his mother went to London practically every day, if not on business, then to see friends or go to the theatre.

Alex was typing when Bruce arrived back in the car, and a few minutes later he knocked at the door of her office and came in.

"What's your programme for this afternoon, Alex?"

"If I finish this before lunch, I've only to take the car to the village to pay in two cheques and collect the flowers your mother ordered. Then I'm free. This really is the pleasantest job."

"You wait. Mother hasn't got you properly on the run yet.

What I came in to suggest, though, was that you came riding with me."

"I'd love to. And I want to see your riding school, too. It must be a nice occupation."

"Not bad, if you've got enough help for the mucky jobs. How good are you?"

"Average."

"That means good, I expect. I'll give you Herod. He's not nearly as fierce as his name, and he'll suit you, I think."

"Haven't you any lessons to give this afternoon?"

"I'm leaving them to Gwen, my assistant. She started as a stable girl, but I guess she can teach 'em all they need to know now. Good enough for the two schoolgirls she's got this afternoon, anyway. Can you be ready by half-past two?"

"Quarter to three."

"O.K. Grand day for a ride."

As Alex ran downstairs buttoning her jacket that afternoon, she met Beth carrying a tray of glasses back to the dining-room. She smiled at Alex as she said,

"I hope you have a nice ride."

She was a timid person and Alex had made little contact with her that week, but she seemed anxious to be friendly.

"I ought to have helped you instead of dashing off to the village directly after lunch," said Alex, feeling guilty, somehow, as she looked at Beth's homely face. She was the only member of the household who seemed to have no fun.

"You have your own job to do. Anyway, Mrs Holloway stays until after lunch on Fridays, and she clears up. I don't trust her with the glasses, though."

"Ready, Alex," said Bruce striding into the hall.

It was a cold, crisp day and they walked to the stables, which were quite close. Alex soon had the feel of Herod, and she shook him up into a canter when they came to the common. Bruce, on a bay gelding, eyed her with approval.

"You'll do," he said, grinning. "Let's make for Winford Heath. Some good gallops there."

Bruce was a fine rider, in complete harmony with his mount,

and when, later on, he challenged her to a race, she was the loser by several lengths.

"Not bad for Herod. He's a bit lazy. I'll claim the prize money later."

They eased the horses to a walk as they turned off the wide gallop and followed a track across the heather leading homewards.

"Does Beth ride? I felt a bit mean, leaving her all alone."

"No. She doesn't like it. She's a funny soul. You don't have to worry. She likes her domestic niche, you know."

"Rather lonely for her, with Juliet away all day at her dancing school."

"Not quite so lonely as you think, perhaps. Can you keep a secret, Alex?"

"Yes."

"Cross your heart?"

"Cross my heart."

"Well, our Beth has a young man. The first of her life. I'm the only one who knows, and there'll be the father and mother of a row if it gets out, so no hints."

"Why should there be a row?"

"Because it's our local garage hand. A young man on the make, if ever I saw one, with quite a reputation among the village maidens. Poor old Beth. She must be cuckoo to think he's after anything but the old man's money."

"That's a little unkind. How did you find out?"

"Well, I've noticed a gentle glow about Beth lately. She's not exactly a vivacious type, and a stranger wouldn't have noticed, but she's seemed a lot brighter than usual. Then, one day last week, I spotted them walking across the field behind the church, his arm round her waist. They didn't see me. I was walking a horse down the lane. He'd gone lame. I saw them through a gateway."

"It could be a genuine attachment. Beth is very sweet, and so domesticated. I'm sure your mother would be sympathetic about it."

Bruce chuckled.

"We'll see. It may not come to anything. Our young Don

Juan may not be able to stay the course, but believe me, he's on the wrong horse if he thinks Dad's purse strings would ever be opened for him."

"I haven't met your father yet. He and Nigel seem very elusive."

"Father often stays at his club in London when he's busy. His business headquarters are in the city, you know, although he travels all over the home counties keeping an eye on his precious shops. He's branching out in other directions now, though, and he's in London more than ever. It suits us."

"Why?"

"He's a bit grim, sweetheart. Quite civilised and all that, but thinks of nothing but business and somehow casts a gloom over the family unless Mother's there to mask it. She's staying in London this evening for a theatre, though, and leaving us to bear the brunt of the old man for dinner. He'll be home tonight. He may make a special effort if you're there, though."

"He sounds a bit alarming."

"He doesn't bother us much," said Bruce airily, as they came out into the lane which led to the stables.

"And nor does Nigel, apparently. All I've seen of him has been the back of his car going out in the mornings. He seems to live like a hermit in the lodge."

"He's breaking bread with us tomorrow, Saturday being Ben's day off."

"I rather like Ben. I met him cycling home from the village one afternoon. Judging from the contents of that huge basket he has in front of his bike, Nigel was in for a good dinner."

"You bet he was. Ben was a chef in a Soho restaurant before he joined Nigel."

They were back at the stables and Bruce handed the horses over to a young woman he addressed as Jackie, and then showed Alex round. He owned a dozen horses, and a two-acre paddock with some jumps.

"It's not a bad life," he said amiably, in answer to Alex's enquiry. "I do a bit of show jumping myself, which adds to the excitement. Suits me, anyway. The old man would have liked me to devote myself to his little business empire, but that would drive me round the bend. Deadly grim. There are easier ways of earning the comforts of life than that. I'm not interested in the commercial jungle, and I like a bit of freedom. The old man's a slave to work. Die of thrombosis or ulcers at an early age, I shouldn't wonder."

Alex, looking at his lithe figure and glowing face, could not imagine him shut up in a London office. His blue eyes, rather paler than his mother's but with the same bright alertness, met hers and he smiled his recognition of her appraisal. He must have met such admiration often, she thought, blushing faintly as she said,

"I couldn't bear to work in a London office, either. That's why I'm so pleased with this job. I have plenty of freedom, and Bridgefield still has a lot of open country."

"We've a great deal in common. I knew it as soon as I saw you. What do I get for winning that race?"

They were standing near a brushwood jump, and he drew her behind it.

"What do you suggest?" she asked.

He smiled as he took her in his arms and kissed her.

"Don't look so startled," he said afterwards. She had her hands against his chest and he covered them with his own. "Life's for enjoying, Alex."

"You must think I'm a very green girl."

"Do you really want to know what I think?"

"Yes."

"That your lack of sophistication is the most refreshing thing I've come across for years, and that Mother's choice of secretary is the most marvellous bit of luck for all of us, and for me in particular. I don't mind admitting that I was feeling pretty bored with the picture of this new year when you came along and opened up a most delightful prospect."

"What might that be?"

"Why, of educating you in ways of enjoyment that somehow, and to me that's inexplicable, have passed you by."

"You know, you and your mother are both a little overwhelming. You sweep me off my feet and leave me breathless."

"Doesn't it feel nice, to be swept off your feet?"

"Very," she replied, her cheeks dimpling, and he kissed her again before putting his arm round her shoulders and piloting her round the jump, when they both stopped abruptly. Leaning negligently against the five-barred gate which formed the next jump was a man in a grey tweed overcoat, smoking a cigarette. He straightened up when he saw them and walked across.

"What are you doing, lurking about like an M.I. man, Nigel?" asked Bruce, grinning as they met.

"That's what I get for being tactful. I looked in to see if you were available, saw your back and another go into the paddock, and followed you, not realising that you had important business to attend to behind the hurdle. Being a perfect gentleman, I waited until you were free. Introduce me, Bruce."

"Miss Madison, Mother's new secretary. You may call her Alex. Allow me to present the owner of the car you see every morning, Alex. Dr. Nigel Lynton, my half-resident half-brother."

Alex was glad of the dusk to hide her flushed face as she shook hands with the newcomer. There was something in his deep-voiced drawl and mocking attitude that made the situation far more embarrassing than if he had interrupted their embrace. Bruce, however, was in no way perturbed. He took Alex's arm again as they walked back, while Nigel explained further.

"Mother telephoned just before I left. She'd been trying in vain to get Beth at home or you here, but nobody answered anywhere. She was really quite affronted."

"We left Beth at home earlier this afternoon," said Bruce. "What did Dorinda want?"

"To tell you not to meet her at the station tonight. She's going to a supper party after the theatre and staying with friends for the night, so she'll be home tomorrow morning, and will somebody kindly be at the station at 11.35."

"O.K.," said Bruce. "What brings you away from the test-tubes so early? It's only just half-past four."

"I've an appointment with Guy Carstairs and the builder in

Elton at five, and I'm going on to the Carstairs' for dinner afterwards. That's why I hoped to catch you here and save time, or so I mistakenly hoped," concluded Nigel dryly.

"Too bad," said Bruce. "Have the plans for your house been finally approved?"

"Not yet. We hope to hammer out the last little problems tonight."

"I bet you're a fussy customer. Good thing Guy's a friend of yours."

They had reached the stable entrance and Nigel made for his car, saying,

"So long, Miss Madison. 'Bye, Bruce. So sorry to have intruded."

In the near darkness, Alex had gathered a rather sinister impression of this tall man with the lean, sallow face and dark eyes. As she watched the car drive away, she felt that he was an extremely unlikeable person and was glad that he was so detached from the Raynham household. She detested people who used irony to make others feel foolish.

"Well, well. Now you've met the elusive tenant of the lodge."

"He's very different from the rest of you, thank goodness."

Bruce chuckled.

"You didn't take to him?"

"I thought him detestable. I'm sorry. Perhaps I shouldn't say that."

"Why not? Your frankness is what I find so attractive. He's a difficult devil, anyway. He's written us off as a useless bunch, you know."

"That doesn't make me like him any more."

"You mustn't stand around and get cold. Come into the office while I have a word with Jackie and Gwen, and close up."

It was quite dark by the time they walked up the lane together, arm in arm, and a crescent moon had appeared over the trees. Alex said little, her thoughts a confusion of happiness and amazement that her staunch citadel of independence could have been stormed so rapidly and so completely by Bruce

Raynham. When he squeezed her shoulder and said "Dear Alex" just before opening the door for her, she felt in such a melting state that she wondered if her legs would carry her up the stairs.

Although Bruce had made his father's presence at dinner sound something of an ordeal, Alex found Mr Raynham more agreeable than she had expected. He was a striking-looking man, tall and broad-shouldered, with greying hair but with a vigour about him that denied his years. He looked formidable, certainly, with thin lips and an unusually long chin, but there was a certain charm about his smile, and he went out of his way to be pleasant to Alex. He took his coffee into his study after dinner, however, and they saw no more of him that evening.

Bruce went out after dinner, and Alex stayed in the drawing-room writing a letter to her family while Juliet curled up in the armchair with a magazine. Beth had disappeared.

"Well, I'm bothered. Here's a photograph of Barney," said Juliet, studying a page of the magazine more closely.

"Your fiancé?" asked Alex, turning.

"M'm. Want to see?"

Over Juliet's shoulder, Alex looked for John Barnabas among the group of men photographed at a dinner party, but none of the men seemed to Alex to be young enough to be Juliet's fiancé.

"That's Barney, with all those medals," said Juliet, her finger on a rather portly man with a small, black moustache.

Alex tried to hide her surprise and said,

"How long have you been engaged, Juliet?"

"Since October. We're planning to be married in June. He's a perfect pet."

Alex looked at the hoop of diamonds on Juliet's finger and wondered why such a lovely girl should be drawn to a staid, dull-looking man so many years her senior. But then love was a funny thing, thought Alex. Girls seemed to marry the most unlikely men and to be happy with them. She looked at Barney again. Perhaps the photograph did not do him justice. Flash-lights were apt to make one look vacuous.

"I'm glad I shall be here for the wedding. You'll be a lovely bride, Juliet."

"How sweet of you! I'll be able to introduce you to Barney next week. He's due back from Germany on Wednesday. Been over there on business for ten days. He travels a lot."

"Will you travel with him when you're married?"

Juliet wrinkled up her nose and snuggled into the cushions like a contented kitten.

"I don't think so. I should only be in the way. I shall be sitting at home waiting for him like a good little wife in a home as lovely as I can make it."

"Have you decided where you'll live?"

"In London. I'm not a country lover, and Barney likes living in London, too. We're looking out for a house now. I rather fancy Hampstead or Chelsea."

She seemed to have it all worked out quite happily. It must be nice to be as sure of everything as that, thought Alex, whose life had never run on such smooth, even lines. Juliet returned to her magazine and Alex went on with her letter. Home seemed somehow a little remote, and it struck Alex as she wrote that she had not felt homesick for a moment since her arrival here. The family, bless them, seemed a little tame beside the liveliness of the Raynham household. How Grandma Madison would have enjoyed these gay, attractive people! For all her age, the flame had never ceased to burn brightly in her spirit, and Alex felt a pang at the thought of her, and realised, too, that it was a whole week since that grief had stirred in her heart. She had been absolutely right to come here, and her grandmother would have been the first to approve, she concluded, as she finished her letter with further reassurances and sealed it.

"I think I'll just walk down the lane and post this now," she said.

"It's a cold night. I wouldn't turn out. It won't get there any sooner than if you post it tomorrow."

"True enough, but I feel like a walk. I'll take old Bella. It'll cheer her up."

"What energy!"

"I know. My family think I'm a terrible fidget. Never was good at sitting still for long."

Bella, the sad-looking black spaniel, who seemed to receive very little attention from anybody, wagged her stump so furiously when she saw Alex pick up her lead that her fat old body swayed like a drunkard's. Old age and an inactive life had made Bella a slow mover, however, and their progress to the pillar box was leisurely. Alex, with plenty of time to think, reflected that it was scarcely credible that only a week had elapsed since her arrival at Pelham House. Already she felt intimate with all the family, except Nigel, who didn't count, and instead of being a new employee, she seemed to have been absorbed by the Raynhams as though they had known her all her life. Next time she went riding with Bruce, she would ask for that grey colt, and see if she could win the race. Then she wondered if she really did want to be the winner.

"Bella," she said, as she stooped to remove the lead as soon as they were inside the gates of Pelham House, "I don't know what's happened to me. I'm thoroughly demoralised. My puritanical instincts have gone with the wind. But isn't it exciting?"

Bella, however, bent on exploring the frosted lawn, nose to ground, was perhaps too old to be a sympathetic confidante.

Chapter Four

"ALEX, would you be an angel and type a few letters and an article for me this afternoon? I know it's a shame to ask you to work on a Saturday afternoon, but they really should go off this week-end."

"Of course, Mrs Raynham. I've had a lot of free time this week, anyway."

"You'll find me just a wee bit naughty about working hours," said Mrs Raynham, smiling ruefully. "But I have so many calls on my time that I can't tie myself down to fixed hours."

"Like theatres and luncheon dates," said Bruce, grinning.

"My social contacts are all part of my job, darling. How handsome you look in riding kit, Bruce! Have you got a lot of pupils this afternoon?"

"A hacking party to conduct. So long, girls."

He patted his mother's shoulder and ruffled Alex's hair as he passed behind them.

"Such a dear boy, Bruce," said his mother complacently. "Always so lively and good-humoured. I do like cheerful people about me. Now, dear, let's get to work."

When Alex took Bella for a walk that evening, Bruce went with her.

"Can't have you walking the countryside alone on a dark night. Mother thinks it's highly dangerous."

"Heavens, I'm used to walking in the country at all hours. You know, I'm surprised at your mother living here. She seems so much a townswoman."

"She is. It was a passing mood she had for living in the country, as long as it was within daily reach of London. I influenced her choice a bit. I like the country. I feel like a chicken in a coop in London. So Bridgefield seemed a sensible compromise. My father fancied a country house for entertaining, too. We don't do as much of that as we used to, thank goodness. His business associates are pretty grim, but Mother puts her spell on them."

"She really is a marvellous person. I don't see how anybody could resist her."

"She usually carries all before her. Will you come riding with me tomorrow, Alex?"

"I'd love to."

"Do you always accept invitations so eagerly?"

"No. Often in the past, I've tried to dodge them."

"I'm favoured, then."

"Yes," she said simply. "I feel happy and at home with you.

I've never felt like that with men before. In fact, I've rather scorned them. You're different."

"How delightfully naïve you are!"

"Is it embarrassing for you?"

"Not a scrap. You're the greatest fun in the world."

"Can I have the grey colt tomorrow, Bruce?"

"No. You might beat me, and I like the prize money too much for that."

"I'd love to try him. He looks so lively."

"He's a bit of a handful. I wouldn't want you to have him until I've schooled him into better manners. You stick to Herod and pay up nicely for your ride, or don't you like paying?"

"Don't tease, Bruce."

He laughed as he put his arm round her waist and drew her close. A moment later they were caught in the headlights of an approaching car, and Bruce drew her into the hedge as it swept past and turned into the drive of Pelham House just ahead of them.

"Lord Nigel," said Bruce. "I want to have a word with him."

"Then I'm off," said Alex promptly, but he caught her as she made to run ahead.

"Kiss me good night."

In the light streaming from the lodge window, he cupped her face between his two hands and kissed her mouth twice. Then he twisted her round and gave her a playful little smack to speed her on her way as he said, "Good night, pet. Happy dreams."

"Good night, Bruce."

She whistled Bella and ran up the drive just as Nigel emerged from the garage. She sped past him without a word, the spaniel lumbering along behind her. In her room, which looked pale and ghostly in the light of the moon shining through the windows, she sought solitude in which to give full rein to her happiness. Her heart was racing and her cheeks burned as she crossed to the window seat and leaned her face against the cool glass. Her desire just then to keep company only with the night was foiled, for Bruce and Nigel were talking in the drive below, and their words came clearly to her through the open ventilator above her head.

"You've not wasted much time in getting to know the red-head, Bruce."

"She's a poppet."

"H'm. Finding the job most agreeable, I'd say."

"She's a jolly nice girl, so there's no need to exercise your devastating wit on low wisecracks."

Nigel laughed and said blandly,

"My dear chap, I shouldn't dream of sullying your fun. She knows her way about, I'm sure."

"What makes you think that?"

"Come now. She's been here for only one week, and yet twice I've turned up inopportunely. Expert though you are, my boy, I'm not young enough to believe that girls don't ask for what they get. Good luck to you. That coloured hair indicates a good return on your money."

"What a cynical old devil you are, Nigel!"

"I know. Sadly lacking in Raynham charm and *bonhomie*. Come in and have a nightcap with me?"

"Thanks, I will. Are you in a hurry for that money?"

"No. Any time."

"O.K. I'll settle up at the end of the month, then."

They moved off to the lodge together, and Alex closed the ventilator, drew the curtains and switched on the light, her mood of trembling happiness swamped in the anger which Nigel's contemptuous words had lit in her. What a loathsome mind he had! She wished now that she had closed the window with a bang to cut off his words, but had hesitated to make her presence known, and then it was too late. He had made her friendship with Bruce sound such a cheap thing, when it was so different. But, thinking of Bruce, her anger fell away. For the first time in her life, she was in love and experiencing all the heady exhilaration which she had condemned in others as foolishness. Sitting on the bed, her hands pressed to her cheeks, it occurred to Alexandra Madison for the first time that her brother might conceivably be right in disapproving of her sweeping judgments.

The next morning, circumstances forced Alex into a meeting with Nigel Lynton which she would have given much to avoid. At breakfast time, it was discovered that Nigel's copy of the *Observer* had been delivered to the house instead of to the lodge, and Mr Raynham, having glanced through it himself, asked Alex if she would be good enough to slip down to the lodge with it. Her intention to push it through the letter-box and avoid any contact with her *bête noire* was foiled by the gentleman himself opening the door at the crucial moment and bidding her good morning. He was dressed in a red and grey silk dressing-gown, which Alex considered both foppish and unbecoming to his dark complexion. It only needed a long cigarette holder to complete the picture, she thought, as she handed him the paper.

"Ah, I was hoping someone would turn up with it before I'd finished my coffee."

"You could have come for it yourself."

"I am not at my strongest early on Sunday morning. If you'll come in, Miss Madison, I'll give you the rag which Juliet likes and which came to me by mistake. Our paper boy is somewhat erratic."

She followed him into a pretty little dining-room, where a blazing fire and an aroma of coffee created a pleasant atmosphere. She missed her coffee in the morning, for the Raynhams preferred tea and nobody had asked her if she had any preference. As though reading her thoughts, he said,

"Can I tempt you to a cup of coffee? Ben's coffee is really good, I assure you."

"I've had my breakfast, thank you. May I have Juliet's paper?"

"A mistake to start Sunday too early," he said. "I'm all for a leisurely start. You look terribly brisk. You're sure you won't have any coffee?"

"Quite."

"You know," he said, pouring a cup for himself, "I feel a very chilly air of disapproval. Why, I wonder?"

This was their first daylight encounter, and Alex eyed coldly the details of the face above the coffee-pot. His black hair receded above his temples to give him a pronounced widower's peak. The eyes which had regarded her so insolently were dark grey, but now they were veiled. The long nose was slightly beaked. He lifted his eyes for a moment, and she noticed again how heavily hooded they were, like a bloodhound's. The whole effect was suave and rather sinister, and reminded her of a satanic illustration of Sherlock Holmes in an old book of her father's.

"Where is Juliet's paper, Dr Lynton?"

"Dear me, we are on our dignity. I shall call you Alex, just to be different. You shall have the paper when you've answered my question."

"I'm not your employee, Dr Lynton. Perhaps you'd send Ben up with it later if it's too far for you to walk yourself."

He was at the door before her, although how he had moved so quickly, she did not know.

"I was right. You did hear what I said last night, then. I saw the light go on in your room, and I thought I heard the window shut just before."

"How very observant you are!"

"My scientific training," he said, grinning. "You're angry with me for that?"

"I haven't liked you from the first moment I saw you, and you must be very obtuse if that surprises you, since you have gone out of your way to be unpleasant."

"Have I? Really, my manners must be slipping. I thought I'd been most polite."

"Sarcasm is polite. It's also poisonous."

He looked at her thoughtfully, his head on one side.

"You're younger than I thought. How old are you?"

"I don't think my age is any business of yours."

"*Much* younger than I thought. Is this your first job away from home?"

"Yes. I worked in my sister's bookshop before this, if you must know."

"You like it here?"

"I like the Raynhams and Pelham House very much indeed," said Alex pointedly, and was annoyed at his smile. He had a skin as tough as an elephant's hide.

"You also like a fight. Will it mollify you if I take back one of my remarks last night?"

"I doubt it."

"Well, in the interests of truth I'll admit that my judgment was wrong in one respect. I said you knew your way around. I was wrong. I think you're a veritable babe in the Raynham wood. I apologise for my error. Due to the dim light and back view, perhaps."

"Thank you. May I have that paper now?"

"In a minute. Must you keep me propped against this door? My coffee's getting cold and I'd feel much happier if you were sitting by the fire."

"I don't want to talk to you or stay here."

"In fact, you can't bear me or my dwelling. Too bad. Do you usually make such quick, decisive judgments?"

"I always know instantly whether I like a person or not."

"Ah, youth," sighed Nigel, looking down at her with the kind of good-humoured tolerance one accorded a puppy. "The black so black and the white so white, and no uncertainties. Grey, I would suggest, is a very common colour, though."

"I have a simple mind," said Alex scathingly.

"I fancy you have an honest one, and that is rare. You're also a rather foolish, self-willed girl, and your parents shouldn't have let you out of their sight."

"How old do you think I am?" asked Alex incredulously.

"I wasn't thinking of years. Early twenties, I suppose."

"I'm twenty-five."

"Thanks for letting me know."

"Oh, you're impossible."

"Well, I don't think I'll let you spoil my coffee any longer."

He fetched the paper from a bureau and handed it to her with a bow.

"My compliments to Juliet and my regrets that she wastes her time on such trash. I know you won't take kindly to any advice from me, but I ought to warn you against taking this family too much to your heart."

"I never listen to malicious talk about my friends. In this case it merely confirms my opinion of you."

He picked up the coffee-pot, saying casually,

"And what has your piercing insight made of three brief encounters, my dear? I know you're pipping to tell me, and I'm always ready to oblige, so fire away."

"I think you're arrogant, vain and malicious, with the typical cold-blooded attitude of a scientist to human beings. We're guinea-pigs for your tongue to dissect, as you dissect animals in your laboratories."

"Ah, the old science versus humanities wrangle. There are no animals in my laboratories, but do go on," he said courteously as he poured cream into his coffee.

"You are also a conceited dandy and I'd like to see you doing some hard physical work, but that might spoil those elegant hands."

"It might," he said seriously. "I could always wear gloves, though. The sad thing is, I'd rather read a book, and let you splendid energetic types work hard at riding and walking the dog and having all kinds of fun and games."

His laughing eyes met hers then and she wished she had something to throw at him.

"And goading people into behaving badly and then laughing at them isn't sporting behaviour, either."

"But I'm not a sport," he said, wiping his eyes. "I'm a dandy. You've just said it. You know, your defence work is shocking. You don't wear your heart on your sleeve, you put it out on a plate, and say, eat it. You'd better come to me for some lessons, or you'll be completely gobbled up."

"I haven't a long enough spoon to sup with the devil," she said, and fled, grasping the paper, hearing his laugh behind her. The fact that she couldn't cope with him made him no more likable.

To her intense annoyance, Nigel, after that meeting, invariably addressed her as babe.

Chapter Five

"MOTHER, before you go into your study, I've some news for you."

"Yes, Beth? What is it, dear? You do look excited."

"Would you like me to go?" asked Alex.

"Of course not, dear," said Mrs Raynham. "You're one of the family now. We've no secrets. I love surprises. Tell me, Beth."

Beth drew in a deep breath, adjusted her glasses a little nervously and said,

"Harry Marksman asked me to marry him last night, Mother. And I said yes."

The smile vanished from Mrs Raynham's face and was replaced with a blank expression which was very rare indeed.

"Harry Marksman? Who is he?"

"Oh, you know, Mother. He works at the garage. Father has him to wash his car sometimes."

Beth's hands were clenched tightly round her table napkin. Breakfast was over, and the others had gone. Mrs Raynham had lingered over the paper, and Alex over a letter from home.

"You don't mean that dark boy with the long black hair?"

"Yes. We've been friendly for some time."

"But, Beth darling, he's years younger than you."

"He's twenty-two. It makes no difference to the way we feel."

"Well, I'm just staggered. Why have you kept it so secret?"

"I was afraid it couldn't be true, and I didn't want to make a fool of myself. But last night . . . We want to get married in March, Mother."

"Now, my dear, you must be sensible about this. I'm not snobbish, heaven knows, but this Harry Marchland . . ."

"Harry Marksman, Mother."

"Harry Marksman, then. What can you have in common with a boy like that? What are you going to live on?"

"We've gone into all that," said Beth eagerly. "That money Grandmother left me. I thought that Father might advance it so that Harry could buy his own business."

"Is this Harry's idea?"

"Of course not. He loves me, Mother. I know that's surprising. I'm nearly thirty, and not . . ." Beth gulped and recovered herself. "But Harry doesn't care about money. He says he earns enough to keep us in a small way, and I'm a good manager. Anyway, we're both terribly happy about it, and nothing anyone says will make any difference."

"Now, darling, don't misunderstand me. It's your happiness I'm concerned about. Nobody would be more delighted than I to see you happily married, and you'll make some man a splendid wife. But this seems such an odd choice of yours."

"I'm not likely to have a lot of choice, Mother."

"Now if you're going to spill that inferiority complex of yours over me, I'm not going to listen," said Mrs Raynham gaily. "And I'm the last person to spread gloom and despondency. We'll have a talk with Father tonight, Beth. He knows Harry better than I do. If he approves, then I shall be reassured and we'll have your young man up and plan a party to celebrate."

Beth's smile was radiant and tremulous.

"Oh, Mother, bless you. I knew if you were on our side, everything would be all right."

"Now, darling, I'm not all-powerful. But don't you worry. It's your happiness we want, after all. Perhaps you'd better let me tell Father first, on my own."

"Yes, that will be best. I'm not good at expressing myself, and Father always makes me feel so stupid."

"Well, we've a lot to do this morning, Alex, so we'd better make an early start. Don't worry, Beth dear. Everything will be all right, I'm sure."

For all her bright reassurances to Beth, Mrs Raynham's frequent spells of preoccupation that morning indicated that her mind was working on other problems than journalistic ones. At midday, she broke off and asked Alex to cancel her luncheon appointment with David Barling.

"Ask him to make it the same time tomorrow, Alex, will you? Tell him that urgent business has taken me to London. Then if you could drive me to the station straight away, I can catch the twelve-thirty and have coffee and sandwiches in the refreshment car. I just can't bring my mind to bear on the *Journal* today, and I'd be worse than useless to David."

"Right. I'll telephone him now," said Alex, picking up the receiver. She was still waiting for her introduction to the editor, but this did not seem an opportune moment to suggest it.

During the next hectic twenty minutes, Alex gathered that Mrs Raynham was going to telephone her husband as soon as she got to London, and arrange to call for him at his office at five, if he could not see her before.

"I can fill in the time with some shopping. I saw an advertisement for a very pretty afternoon dress at Harrods. Then I can have a quiet talk with Leonard in his office before we catch the train home."

"Do you think he'll be against Beth's marriage with this young man?"

"He may," said Mrs Raynham regretfully. "It isn't at all suitable, I'm afraid. But everyone is entitled to happiness, and if it would make Beth happy . . . She's such a sweet girl. I'm sure she deserves the best."

Driving home past the garage, Alex noticed a dark young man at the petrol pump. He was good-looking, in a rather flashy way, but not, Alex thought, the type to inspire the confidence of Mr Raynham.

Dinner that evening was an uneasy function. Gaily as Mrs Raynham chattered, Alex felt the tension there, and she noticed Beth's hand trembling as she cut some bread. Nigel's presence helped to keep the conversation going. Alex wondered whether he knew about Beth and Harry Marksman. He had the sort of eyes that missed very little, she felt, in spite of his suave air of detachment.

By the time they had reached their coffee, Beth could bear it no longer, and said breathlessly,

"Father, has Mother told you about Harry and me?"

"Yes, my dear. A great surprise, I must say. We'll have a talk about it in my study after dinner."

"I'd sooner discuss it here, with the rest of the family. After all, it's not a private affair."

She was frightened of her father, thought Alex, and needed the rest of the family for protection.

"As you wish, Beth."

"What's this all about?" asked Juliet, spooning sugar into her coffee.

"Harry Marksman and I are going to be married," said Beth, her cheeks flushed, her hands tightly clenched.

The silence was broken by Juliet's peal of laughter, which stopped suddenly as she saw Beth's scarlet face.

"You're joking, Beth," she said lamely.

"Why should I be? Is it so funny that I should get married?"

"Of course not," stammered Juliet. "But he's only a boy. A boy with a pretty lively reputation among the girls, too."

"That's all over. He wants to settle down."

Juliet shrugged her shoulders and was silent.

"My dear," said Mr Raynham, "you must try to be practical about this."

"Why?" flashed Beth. "It isn't a practical thing. We love each other and we're going to be married."

"And what do you propose to live on, and where do you propose to live? Young Marksman lives in lodgings somewhere in the village, I believe," said her father laconically.

"I thought . . ." Beth looked at her mother appealingly, but Mrs Raynham was studying her coffee. "That money Grandmother left me. We thought that would be enough to buy a business for Harry. He's very good at his job. And we could probably live over the business."

"But your grandmother didn't leave you any money outright. I explained it all to you at the time, Beth."

"I don't understand all this talk about trusts. I gathered the money was for my benefit. I've never thought much about it before. I haven't needed it. Isn't it available for me?"

Her father spoke slowly and patiently.

"Your grandmother left a certain amount of capital in investments. She appointed me the trustee of these funds. The interest from them was to be paid to you as long as you remained unmarried. If you never married, the interest would be yours for life. The capital was never yours. When you married, it was to go to certain specified charities which I won't bore you with. You knew all this, Beth. I told you myself."

"I . . . I'd misunderstood. I thought you were just looking after it for me."

Her father sighed.

"I sometimes wonder whether you give your mind to anything I say. Your grandmother merely wanted to provide you with a small independent income as long as you remained here and kept house for us. She thought it would be compensation for not earning money in an outside job. She had the old-fashioned idea, however, that a husband maintains his wife, and she wanted her money to go to charities, once you were married. Have you led this young man to think that the capital was yours?"

"Yes."

"Well, that explains it."

"Why do you say that?" asked Beth, her voice shaking. "It will make no difference to Harry. It means we'll have to change our plans, that's all."

"Darling," said her mother, "I do think you'd better talk this over with Harry, and see what he says."

"You think he's only marrying me for my money, don't you? All of you. I'm too old and unattractive for any man to want to marry me. That's what you're all thinking. Well, it's not true. You'll see."

By now the tears were streaming down Beth's face, and her mother went round to her and took her in her arms. Mr Raynham looked on grimly.

"Now, darling, don't upset yourself. It may all turn out for the best. After all, to be married for money can bring much unhappiness, and I must say I've heard one or two things about this boy that make me doubt whether he's the right person to have our Beth."

"You think it's all over, don't you? I'll go and fetch Harry now. And you'll see."

"I think that would be unwise, Beth," said her father.

"Why?"

His lips tightened. He had a lot of work to do, and he hated domestic scenes. Barbara had always kept the peace, leaving him free to concentrate on his work, and now this girl, with her stupid, romantic illusions, was threatening the whole household with chaos. Barbara had left him in no doubt about that. He decided that the time had come to be ruthless.

"Because I don't want to see you humiliated. Be your age, Beth. Harry Marksman is a shrewd, good-looking chap, who's pursued by half the village girls. You're years older than he is, and not his type at all. For heaven's sake, don't behave like a silly schoolgirl."

"*You* don't want to see me humiliated. Who is humiliating me? I'm going to fetch Harry, and I want you all to stay here. He's waiting in the lane. I arranged to meet him there at eight."

She rushed out, and Nigel let out a groan.

"Oh, lord. Poor old Beth."

"Well, we'd best get it over and done with," said Mr Raynham.

"You don't suppose there could be anything genuine in it?" asked Bruce.

"Of course not," said Juliet. "He's a spry young man, that one. Given me the glad eye many times. Really, old Beth is a noodle."

"She's too old to make this kind of a fool of herself," said Mr Raynham coldly.

"Poor darling. I do feel so sorry for her," said Mrs Raynham.

Alex was casting about for an excuse to leave them, for she felt that she had no place in this unhappy family affair, but Beth returned very quickly, leading by the hand the dark young man Alex had glimpsed that morning. He must have been waiting close by. Looking at him more closely, her heart ached for Beth. He was a slender young man, with black, wavy hair which was heavily brilliantined, and a fresh complexion. His dark brown eyes looked a little warily at them above his smiling mouth. He wore a striped tie and a navy blue suit, and looked as alert as a boxer who knows exactly what he is up against.

"Good evening, Harry," said Mr Raynham pleasantly. "Let me introduce you to my family."

This done, he waved Harry to a chair and offered him a cigarette. Beth sat down on the edge of a chair opposite him, her eyes bright and defiant behind her glasses.

"Now, my boy, Beth has told us that you want to marry her, and that you propose to buy a business with the money her grandmother left her. I'm cutting the frills and speaking plainly. Is that correct?"

"Well, more or less. Nothing cut and dried, you understand. Beth told me just now that there's some hitch about the money."

Mr Raynham explained the situation to him.

"I'm afraid my daughter unwittingly misled you, Harry. She should have known the position. I've explained it to her more than once, but I think perhaps her head has been in a whirl lately. I'm sorry if she raised false hopes."

He spoke in a calm, friendly manner, and Alex felt that he, too, knew exactly what he was doing, and it wasn't very nice.

"It won't make any difference," said Beth fiercely.

"My dear, don't force Harry into an awkward position. He's a sensible chap. He knows that you can't live on air. He's young, and I'm sure will do well enough to support a wife in the future, but I'd say that time has not come yet. Don't you agree, Harry?"

"Well, yes. I don't earn a lot at the garage. Not that I intend to stop there, though. I'm not being a garage hand all my life, Mr Raynham. You can bet your bottom dollar on that."

"I'd be ready to risk more than a dollar on that, my boy. You're a smart chap. I've always thought so. But family responsibilities can hold you back, you know, if you take them on prematurely."

"You wouldn't be interested in putting up some capital yourself, Mr Raynham?"

"I'm afraid not, Harry."

He spoke almost regretfully, but their eyes met, and Harry Marksman knew that line was dead.

"Well, Beth, old girl, this does make a bit of difference, you know. If your family would help, we might risk it, but on my own, it's going to mean a long wait, I guess."

"Oh no, Harry. I'm not afraid of being poor. I can get a job, too."

"Beth, darling, you're not qualified," said her mother.

"Don't worry, Mrs Raynham. I shouldn't ask your daughter to do that. I know the sort of life she's been used to. I'm too fond of her to ask her to lower her standard of living for me."

"I knew you'd got a sound head on your shoulders," said Mr Raynham. "If and when you feel in a position to keep Beth and maintain a home, then, of course, there can be no objection to your marrying. But I'm like Beth's grandmother, Harry. I believe in young people making their own way. You would both be on your own, completely. I must make that quite clear."

"I understand, Mr Raynham."

"Harry, don't listen to them. It's my life. If I don't care . . ."

"Beth, try to have a little dignity. You've misled Harry about your prospects, and now you're trying to put pressure on him to commit an act of folly which would have disastrous results for both of you. No young man can climb up from nothing with a wife and children on his back. For heaven's sake, girl, give him a chance. You've led a sheltered life and know nothing of the struggle to make a decent living. Harry knows all about it, and so do I." Her father's eyes were like cold, grey stones as he looked at her.

"How can you be so cruel? Don't feelings come into this at all?"

"My dear, romance is fine for dreaming. You can still have

your dreams. The future may make them come true. I'm
not making any prophecies. I'm only saying that now is not
the time to enter into commitments. You must leave Harry to
be the judge of that."

Beth, suddenly quiet, looked across at Harry and said
gently,

"Well, Harry?"

As she watched him, her face seemed to shrink and her eyes
died. She read his answer before he spoke.

"He's right, old girl. Don't look so unhappy. There's
always the Pools, you know."

"Well, let's all have a drink and cheer up," said Mrs Raynham, going to the cocktail cabinet.

Beth looked round at them for a moment, then turned and
ran out of the room. Mr Raynham sighed.

"I'm afraid she's a little strung up, Harry. I'm sorry if she's
read more into all this than she ought. She's a good girl, but
has never been used to attentions from young men. If your
friendship has gone to her head a little and put you in something of a predicament, you must forgive her. It's only natural
that she should be anxious to marry, after all. What will you
drink?"

In a few minutes, they were all chatting and laughing over
their drinks as though nothing had happened. Only Nigel
said little, standing apart and surveying them all with a faint
smile as he sipped his liqueur brandy. Alex, distressed at Beth's
humiliation, listened to Juliet twitting Harry and wondered
for the first time whether hearts in the Raynham family were
kept in cold storage. Then she told herself that no good would
be served by sitting around with long faces, and Beth had
undoubtedly been saved from a match that could never have
brought her happiness, for if there was one thing that stood
out a mile, it was that Harry Marksman loved Harry and
nobody else. Much better to dismiss the whole grisly business
with a surface friendliness which saved unpleasantness.

Beth did not appear again that evening, having retired
behind a locked door. When Harry had gone, Mrs Raynham
gave a sigh of relief.

"Well, thank goodness that's over. Leonard, you handled it wonderfully."

"Thanks, my dear. Now I must get down to some figures."

"Bruce, pour me another Cointreau, darling," said Mrs Raynham. "Then I'll go and fetch the dress I bought at Harrods this afternoon to show you, Juliet. It's simply lovely. A dove grey silk with chiffon panels. I bought a sweet little blouse for Beth, too. I'll take it to her. It'll cheer her up, perhaps."

And at this, Nigel broke into a laugh.

"Mother, you really are priceless. A broken heart mended by a blouse from Harrods. God's in his heaven and all's right with the world, as long as we can have our frills."

"You'd be surprised what an effect they have on morale, my boy. It's nice to have you here, Nigel. Why don't you come in more often?"

"Swop the peace of my own table for this sort of domestic rough and tumble? Not on your life."

"Well, tonight was an exception. When will Ben be back?"

"On Friday. His sister's funeral is tomorrow, and he's staying on with his brother-in-law for a day or two."

"Don't talk about funerals. I wish I could persuade domestics to give me the service Ben gives you. How do you manage to keep him, Nigel? Shamefully over-paying, I suppose."

"Ben wouldn't thank you for referring to him as a domestic."

"Well, what else is he? He cooks and looks after the lodge for you. Mrs Holloway says he's dreadfully fussy about the place, too. He'll offend her if he's not careful, and then he'll have to polish the floors himself."

"Ben's a good diplomat."

"Fetch your dress, Mother. I'd love to see it," said Juliet.

Alex decided that someone would have to clear the dining-table, since Beth had retired, and she began to stack the things on the trolley.

"Oh, thank you, Alex," said Mrs Raynham. "Just leave it all in the kitchen. It can wait until tomorrow."

Leave it to Beth to tackle in the morning, thought Alex a

little grimly. She had started washing the glasses when Nigel joined her in the kitchen.

"Hullo, babe. Good idea. I'll join the fatigue party. I'm not in the mood for a fashion show."

"What a dreadful evening for Beth! I do think they might have thought of her feelings a little more. Mr Raynham made it sound as though she'd hounded Harry Marksman down and done him a disservice."

"M'm. Masterly, wasn't it? Have to hand it to my stepfather. If he'd been aggressive with Harry and put his back up, he might have married Beth out of spite. As it was, he made the young man feel a victim, bolstered up his ego by some well-placed flattery, made it quite clear that not one penny of Raynham money would reach his eager hands, and finished up good pals. An object lesson in how to impose your will on others with kid gloves."

"And poor Beth! *She* wasn't handled with kid gloves."

"She wasn't the one who mattered."

"Don't. You make it sound so cold-blooded. After all, they have saved Beth from wrecking her life. That young man would never have made her happy. He was only out for his own ends."

"Quite. It was a foolish business, all right. Poor old Beth. She's nearly thirty, and never had a boy friend in her life. A bit hard, with Juliet drawing them like bees to honey."

"And Beth's such a good, kind person. And very competent. Mr Raynham treats her as though she's a fool just because she doesn't understand money matters, but she's a splendid housekeeper and that's a job that needs intelligence."

"Yes. A pity for Beth, perhaps, that she is so good at it."

"Why?"

"My dear babe, have you considered what a priceless asset Beth is to my mother?"

"Yes," said Alex doubtfully.

"She takes all the household responsibilities off her shoulders and allows her to dabble in her journalism, go off to London, live the life of a bachelor woman, with all the home comforts for her and her family taken care of. In these days of the disappearance of domestic help, except for the odd daily, Beth is absolutely indispensable to Mother's way of life."

"That's true, but I don't see the connection."

"Why, even if Beth found the most suitable husband in the world, Mother would fight tooth and nail to break it up. She stands to lose too much."

"I don't believe it. She's far too kind. She was only saying this morning that she'd be delighted to see Beth married to the right man."

"If you're going to take literally all the words spoken in this house, babe, you're going to get awfully tangled up. It's more often than not double talk which needs interpreting to the uninitiated. Call me in when you need an interpreter. I'm an expert, having lived with it for many of what the psychologists assure us are our most impressionable years."

"You're not exactly loyal, are you?"

"Oh, cut the schoolgirl stuff," he said impatiently. "We're talking about truth and lies, what's underneath the curtain of talk. Not schoolgirl loyalties."

"Your mother was very concerned about Beth spoiling her life by marrying someone who was no good," said Alex coldly.

"And I'm saying that it would be all the same, no matter who the chap was. I hold no brief for young Marksman. I think he's a smart Alec and Beth would be a mug to marry him, but that isn't the important thing where Mother is concerned."

"What is, then?"

"Why, Mother. Haven't you learnt that yet? I bet she let herself go with my stepfather this afternoon. She prefers to get someone else to do the dirty work."

"I still think you've a horrible mind that suspects everybody's motives."

He shrugged his shoulders.

"I'm not sitting in judgment. Just stating the truth. I admire Dorinda in many ways. But it doesn't do to let your heart get involved with her, babe, or with any of the Raynhams. They're apt to treat it like a pretty coloured ball off a Christmas tree. They play with it so prettily as long as it amuses them and doesn't get in the way. Like kittens. Just play along with them, and you'll be all right."

"I've told you before, I prefer to make my own judgments."

"Those sweeping black and white things? Well, well, I can see I'm going to get no credit for trying to save your skin. Be eaten, my child, and don't say I didn't warn you. Give me credit, at least, for using my elegant hands for wiping up. This cloth's sopping. Do you suppose there's another somewhere?"

He was back in his mocking mood, and she took a dry cloth from the drawer, saying,

"I'll finish off, thank you."

"Don't mention it. Hullo, Juliet, my pretty one. Just too late for the chores, as usual."

"It's nice to see you being useful for a change, anyway. Alex, Mother says you simply must come and see her dress. And she's got the prettiest silk scarf for you."

As Alex followed Juliet out, Nigel gave her a polite bow. He followed them into the drawing-room to say good night to his mother, and then left them. Alex was glad that he had gone. He created an uneasy atmosphere. When Bruce tied the sweater scarf round her neck and kept his hands on her shoulders as he turned her for the approval of the others, she forgot Nigel and warmed once again to the gaiety and goodwill of these Raynhams.

Chapter Six

IN the weeks that followed, Harry Marksman's name was not mentioned. The subject was closed. Beth went about the house with her usual quiet competence, but she looked plainer than ever under a mask of blankness, and Alex found her reserve unbreakable.

Early in February, Bruce took Alex to a dance in Elton, and Juliet and Barney went with them. Further acquaintance with

Juliet's fiancé had not dimmed Alex's first impression of dull stolidity, and, although he was obviously a very kind, good person, it still seemed an odd match for a lovely girl like Juliet Raynham. They seemed happy enough together, however. He was obviously tremendously proud of Juliet and she treated him with playful affection.

Alex, not a particularly good dancer, found Barney's unambitious jog-trot style of dancing fairly comfortable, and he had several dances with her while Juliet was carried off by various young men. She was a lovely dancer, and was well known as the assistant teacher at the Elton School of Dancing, so that it was small wonder that she was in such demand, thought Alex when Barney asked her for yet another dance before Bruce could claim her. Barney was evidently not going to dance with strangers. When he apologised for treading on her toe, Alex smiled and said,

"I expect I was to blame. I'm not a good dancer. I prefer the Scottish reels and old time dances where I can let myself go."

"Can't stand dancing myself," confided Barney with a sheepish smile which Alex found rather endearing, "but with Juliet so good at it, I shall have to keep my end up by going to a few, I guess."

Bruce, having sized up the situation, swept Alex off more promptly as the evening wore on, and she found herself dancing better than ever before.

"Not having you monopolised by old Barney," said Bruce, as he drew her off the floor to a quiet alcove in the refreshment lounge.

She chose a soft drink, and Bruce sat down beside her with his own gin and tonic, watching her sip her orange squash through a straw while she looked at the dancers. When her eyes turned to him, she flushed a little under his affectionate scrutiny.

"You look about ten," he said, "and I could eat you."

This was too reminiscent of Nigel's gloomy forebodings, she thought, and then quivered as Bruce slid an arm round her back and rested his hand on her bare shoulder.

"I thought this dress made me look particularly sophisticated," she said. "I've never had a dance frock that left my shoulders bare before. I think I'm a bit skinny for it, as a matter of fact."

"You have a pearly skin that's as smooth as silk, and your neck and shoulders are quite delightful. It would be a shame to hide them. But you haven't a sophisticated face, sweetheart. It's as open and candid as a sunny field. That's how I like it, too."

"Juliet's the belle of the ball, isn't she? Barney's so proud of her. He hardly spoke of anything else while we were dancing."

"Yes. She's going to be the indulged little wife all right. Trust Juliet."

"I think he's a lucky man. She's so lovely. He must be years older than she is."

"He's forty-three. Decorated in the last war. A nice chap. A good match for Juliet, you know. He's worth a cool two millions."

"Yes, but . . ." She stopped. The disparity in age between Harry Marksman and Beth had made Juliet laugh. This way round, and with a millionaire involved, it didn't seem to matter.

"But what?"

"Oh, nothing. I should have thought Juliet would have preferred a younger, livelier person, but perhaps Barney makes her feel safe and protected," said Alex, wishing these odd, uncomfortable thoughts wouldn't keep popping up with Nigel's mocking face accompanying them, like a Satanic jack-in-the-box.

"Could be. But why are we wasting time talking about my sister? How long is it going to take me to drive you to your home tonight?"

"About half an hour. Are you sure you don't mind, Bruce? I could get a taxi."

"Not on your life. I wish I could have accepted your invitation to stay this week-end, but Sunday is a busy day for me at the stables."

"Yes, I know. Another time, perhaps."

"I shall miss our evening walk tomorrow, though."

"Me, too. But coming so near home as Elton, I felt I ought to take the opportunity to see the family. I've only been back one week-end since I started this job, you know."

"You must like it with us. Do you, Alex?"

"You know I do. Will you take Bella for her walk just the same tomorrow evening, Bruce? She counts on it now."

"If you're nice to me going home."

"I'm always nice to you, aren't I?"

"Very nice," he said, smiling and squeezing her shoulder.

On the way to Alex's home, Bruce drew the car off the road and took her in his arms.

"It's been a lovely evening, Bruce. Thank you so much."

"Lovely for me too," he said, kissing her gently.

She nestled against him as he slid his hand inside her coat and drew her close. She loved him, and as she lifted her face to his, she was filled with such an intense gratitude to him for transforming her life into this wonderful shimmering state of happiness that she struggled in vain for adequate words.

"Bruce . . . I wish I could tell you how much . . ."

Mercifully, he stopped her mouth with his, and reduced her to a slavish acquiescence which turned to eager response before he released her with a shaky laugh.

"Alex, you're going to my head. I feel distinctly drunk. I'll have to light a cigarette to steady my nerves before I drive on, or I might land you in a ditch. You're a most delightful pupil, you know. You tempt me to rush the lessons."

She laid her head on his shoulder while he smoked a cigarette, content to relax and enjoy the comfort of his arm round her waist, his caressing hand, his voice murmuring endearments. She was sorry when he drove on. She would have liked that peaceful bliss to have remained unbroken for ever. He pulled up at the entrance to Camerino and refused her invitation to drive up to the house and come in for a drink.

"Better not, sweetheart. It's nearly one o'clock, and I've a good drive home in front of me. Looks like a nice place," he said appreciatively as he peered out of the car window at the gables of Camerino just visible above the trees.

"It is a nice old house. We all love it, but Clive says we can't afford to keep it up. It's too big for these days."

"Costs a packet to run anything more than a cottage, if you ask me. Have your family owned this for long?"

"Great Grandfather had it built. It would be a pity to have to sell it for a hotel or school or something. Still, Clive's the one who'll have to keep it going after Dad, and he isn't a rich man. Dad has a poor business head, Clive says, and it's more than he can manage now."

"One of you girls will have to marry a millionaire and save the old home," said Bruce lightly.

"Afraid we're not the type. Delia, my eldest sister, runs a hotel and is a confirmed spinster. She had an unhappy love affair and she's never looked at a man since. Rosalind's married a civil engineer. He's not likely to be rich."

"Oh, yes, Ian Langley. I know. We used to see quite a lot of the Langleys. Mrs Langley and Mother went to school together. Lost touch with them in recent years. Well, that only leaves you to retrieve the family home, then, Alex. I'm afraid it's too late to catch Barney."

"Don't, Bruce. You're spoiling the atmosphere with all this talk of money. It doesn't mean a thing to me."

"I should laugh at anyone else who said that, but for you, my dear redhead, I believe it's true, unworldly child that you are."

"Well, I don't want to get out, but I suppose I must."

"Kiss me good night."

"I'll never forget this evening, Bruce," she whispered as she moved her lips from his mouth across his cheek. "Never." Then she slid out of the car, took the small suitcase he handed out to her, and waited at the edge of the lane while he reversed the car into the drive of Camerino. He leaned out and blew her a kiss, and she waved him off, standing there until the tail light of his car disappeared at the end of the lane. Then she walked slowly up the drive between the rhododendron bushes to Camerino. Although she was sorry that he had not come into her home that night, she was sure that the time was not far off when she would lead him into Camerino and introduce him to her family. She knew that they would approve of Bruce. Who could do otherwise? In the meantime, their love could wait, in secret, for the right moment to tell the world.

There was a light in the drawing-room. Her father had probably waited up for her. She hoped that her face would not reveal prematurely what was in her heart, but her love burned so brightly that she thought it must be plain for all to see. . . .

At the end of the month, after Alex had dropped a few hints, she was introduced to the editor of *Downland Journal* at his editorial office in the village. He was older than she had expected, with grey hair and a good-humoured face. Wearing a tweed suit which looked like an old friend, he sat on the corner of his desk, smoking a pipe, while he listened to Mrs Raynham holding forth on the lack of culture in Bridgefield. Alex thought she caught a twinkle in his blue eyes once when he glanced across at her. It was a conspiratorial look, and Alex warmed to him. In her usual decisive manner, she decided that David Barling was her sort of person, and as soon as she could get a word in, she told him how much she liked his two books for young naturalists which she had read years ago, and which were still among her most prized possessions. Catching on to her enthusiasm, he somehow managed to keep the conversation to the two of them for several minutes, no mean feat in Barbara Raynham's company. By the time they left, Alex had arranged to write an article on the countryside in March for his criticism, and she drove Mrs Raynham back to Pelham House in high spirits, convinced that her foot was on the first step of a career in journalism. How fortunate, she thought, that it was a career which could be carried on after marriage! She was sure that Bruce would encourage her efforts.

This interview with Barling revived all Alex's enthusiasm for natural history, which lately had been pushed aside by the all-embracing impact of the Raynhams on her life. Now, after Bella's evening walk, she often changed into slacks and sweater and went out again, armed only with a pocket torch and magnifying glass, to see what was stirring in the country. She could not arouse in Bruce an interest in wild life sufficiently strong to make a silent companion of him on these forays. He maintained that he could not be in her company and behave like a mummy, and a few trial expeditions proved the truth of this assertion, so that, reluctantly, she took to prowling alone, much to the expressed alarm of Mrs Raynham. It was not in her employer's nature to worry unduly over other people's eccentricities, however, and she soon learned to accept Alex's nocturnal explorations.

On one such exploration in March, when the weather was mild and dry after a showery day, she decided to make her way along the ditch at the side of the lane to the spot where, half an hour before, Bella had shown great interest. She was lying flat on her stomach in the long grass when the headlights of a car picked her up, and a frightful screeching of brakes caused her to wince and exclaim in annoyance.

"My dear, are you all right?"

Her eyes travelled up a pair of long legs and a dark overcoat to Nigel's face, pale and anxious in the uncertain light of a cloud-dodging moon.

"Of course I am. I'm just looking at a toad," she said crossly. Car brakes and the peace of the night were not compatible.

"Well, I'm . . ." Then he laughed. "Bless my soul. What a girl you are! I thought you'd been knocked out by a thug."

"How silly! There aren't any thugs round here, and I'm near enough to the house to be heard if I screamed. Now you've disturbed everything. No. There he is." Her voice changed as she shone her torch on a tuft of grass and dead leaves a few feet away. "Look, Nigel," she whispered reverently. "Isn't he a splendid fellow?"

Nigel stooped down and looked at the portly figure of the toad, plodding slowly along at the bottom of the ditch, stopping now and again but apparently not greatly disturbed by their presence.

"He's rather beautiful, isn't he? Such lovely eyes," she added softly.

"Well, beautiful isn't quite the word, perhaps, but he's certainly a well set-up toad."

"He's on his way to a pond for breeding. They'll be spawning now. Isn't it wonderful to think of all the frogs and toads on the move at night making for water and a mate?"

"You're a naturalist, I gather."

"I've always been one, ever since I could walk. It's funny how much happiness it gives you. A different kind of happiness from any other."

"How different?" he asked, straightening his aching knees and looking down at her with an odd smile which she did not notice, for her eyes were still following the toad.

"Oh, peaceful and absorbed, somehow. I can't analyse it. Bother, he's gone under those tree roots. I don't expect he'll come out again until we've gone." She smiled up at him. "Wasn't that interesting?"

"Most," he said gravely and held out his hand to help her up, but she sprang to her feet unaided and brushed the damp leaves and twigs from her sweater and slacks.

"There are some celandines in bloom under the hedge there. Spring's on the way. I must put the toad and the celandines in my article for *Downland Journal*. I wonder if Mr Barling will publish it."

"If you're able to convey your enthusiasm, and it's the sort of thing that usually gets through even an amateurish gift of expression, he probably will."

"How nice and encouraging of you!"

"It's spring in the air. Are you continuing your research, or can I give you a lift back?"

"No, I think I'll go on a little further, thank you."

"Righto. Good hunting."

"It seems awful to be shut up indoors while so many exciting things can be happening out here. Good heavens, Nigel! Your eye. I've only just noticed it."

"It's a beauty, isn't it?"

"What happened? Did you bump into something?"

"I came into contact with the knee of a loutish forward in a rugby match last Saturday."

"Rugger? Do *you* play rugger?"

"Shocking rough game, isn't it? I'm thinking of giving it up after this season. Getting too old."

"It must be very painful," said Alex lamely, feeling that he was enjoying her confusion.

"Not as bad as it looks now. As the colours ripened, the pain lessened."

"It makes you look frightfully sinister in this light."

"But I am sinister, babe, aren't I? You should have been there to see me sullied and knocked about. You'd have enjoyed it."

"You lay traps for people. Why do you pretend to be such a languid fop? You deserve to be misjudged."

He chuckled and laid a paternal hand on her head.

"You rise so beautifully to the bait. Anyway, because I indulge in a sporting occupation sometimes, it doesn't lessen my liking for comfort and a decently civilised way of life. You simplify too much, babe."

"You look a poor example of elegant living with that black eye, anyway," said Alex, laughter in her voice.

"You shall have your little gloat. You've earned it," he said good-humouredly as he opened the car door. "Let me know if you're in the *Journal* and I'll buy a copy."

He was almost nice, thought Alex as he drove off. She had to concede that he was not an easy person to know, but in a few minutes he had faded from her mind as she tried to decide how long to wait concealed by a hole which she suspected might be the entrance to a badger's sett. To avoid search parties, she had better limit herself to half an hour. With her eyes alert, she trod lightly, making no sound in her crêpe-soled shoes as she padded along the lane, climbed a gate into a field, and made for the spinney, on the outskirts of which was the hopeful-looking hole with the tell-tale litter of grass and leaves close by.

Chapter Seven

"How is he?" asked Alex, as she stepped into the hall of the lodge.

"Very touchy," said Ben grimly. "I wouldn't call him a good patient. Very trying today, and that's a fact. But there, 'flu does leave you feeling low."

"I've brought a record he asked me to fetch for him. And here's his change. Perhaps I'd better not see him if he's crotchety."

"Well, he's past the infectious stage, so you don't have to worry about that. Going back to his precious labs tomorrow. But I wouldn't call him a ray of sunshine."

"Ben, what are you nattering about out there? If that's Alex, send her in."

The voice came from the sitting-room, and Alex went in to find Nigel stretched out on the couch in front of a blazing fire, surrounded by a litter of papers covered with figures.

"How are you, Nigel?"

"Pretty well, thanks."

"Here's the record you ordered. And here's your change."

"Thanks, babe. Going to stay and have a cup of coffee with me?"

"Would you like me to?" she asked cautiously.

"Yes. Your bright face cheers me up. I feel like a wet Sunday myself. Tell me what goes on in Pelham House these days. Nothing like a dose of 'flu to keep people at a distance."

"Isn't that what you like?"

"Precisely. But tonight I'm in the mood for idle gossip," he said, gathering together the papers of figures.

"Well, your mother and Juliet are staying in London for a day or two seeing to clothes for the wedding, and inspecting the house Barney's bought at Hampstead. Your mother hasn't seen it yet, and Juliet wants her advice about curtains."

"Well, that should keep them both out of mischief for the next couple of months. Interior decorating goes to Mother's head. I'm not letting her put a foot in my house until it's furnished, complete to the last cushion."

"How's it getting on? Your house."

"Up to the first floor. You must come over and see it some time."

"I'm honoured."

"I can cope with you. Ah, thanks, Ben. You can pour, Alex. Black for me, and no sugar."

"What beautiful coffee cups!"

"M'm. And how's the journalism?"

"Mr Barling's going to publish my article in the April number. It needed a lot of editing, of course. Your mother helped me there. She knows how to be pithy. Bruce is taking me out to dinner tomorrow night to celebrate my first appearance in the *Journal*. We're going to the country club at Furze Hill. Do you know it?"

"Fenner's. Yes, I know it. Very good. Didn't know Bruce was a member. It was you two I heard underneath my window last night, I suppose?"

"Yes. I'm sorry if we disturbed you."

"You might move further up the drive for your dilly dallying. There's a nice shady gap between here and the windows of the house."

"If you're going to be objectionable, I shall go."

"I'm not being objectionable. Merely saying that you'd do me a favour by billing and cooing further off. Sit down, babe. Sit down. Don't be a tiresome little squib. I felt deadly last night, and you didn't help me to sleep, that's all. You're very fond of him, aren't you?"

"Yes. He's coming over to Camerino next Sunday to meet my family. At least, he thinks he'll be able to."

"Congratulations," said Nigel a shade dryly.

"Well, it's not quite time for that yet. Please don't say anything about it, Nigel. It's . . . just in the air."

"Trust me. But you've no doubts yourself?"

She looked at him and smiled, her blue-green eyes, always striking, showing even more depth of colour than he had noticed before.

"No doubts at all. Isn't it wonderful?"

"He's very sound in wind and limb, and a nice, easy-going chap."

"People take advantage of his good nature. This afternoon, for example, he's driven all the way to London Airport to meet some friends who cabled him today giving their time of arrival, just as though he's their chaffeur."

"Who are they?"

"I think Bruce said the name was Dalloway or Galloway. The cable was waiting for him when he came in to lunch, and he bolted a sandwich Beth cut him and went off straight away."

"Eve Dalloway. So she's back, is she?"

"They're old friends of the family, Bruce said."

"Yes. The Dalloways live at The Grange, that enormous place hidden away behind the trees opposite the War Memorial. Old Mrs Dalloway is trying to sell it now. Mr Dalloway died about a year ago and left a fortune to Eve, his daughter. She used some of it in going on a world tour."

"It was Eve, then, who cabled Bruce?"

"I guess so. They're old friends, you know."

"I didn't. Bruce has never mentioned her."

"Well, she's been away nearly a year, and people soon drop out, after all."

"A bit of a cheek, sending for him like that. Still, it's not very nice to come home after a year's absence and have nobody to greet you. I always used to hate it when nobody met me at the station when I came home from school at the end of term. Usually somebody did, of course. Perhaps Miss Dalloway hasn't many friends."

"People with money never lack friends, babe."

He was studying the tip of his cigarette, frowning. Then he looked up, and meeting her gaze, smiled and said,

"Like to hear my record? Beethoven's Pathétique sonata."

"Yes, please. Then I'll have to give Bella her evening walk."

"You take your duties seriously."

"Well, the poor old lady has such a dull life. Her sight's a bit dim and she's getting deaf. I think the little walks

I give her are all she lives for now. I can't let her down."

"Sit there and listen to this, then, and it will go with you when you take Bella out."

"I know. That's the splendid thing about Beethoven, isn't it? So singable. I do like music which leaves me singing."

She sat there in the low chair, her face in shadow, her hair gleaming in the soft light of the lamp behind her, while Nigel put on the record and returned to his couch, stretching himself on it with a contented sigh and clasping his hands behind his head as the first haunting chords filled the room. . . .

* * *

At the country club at Furze Hill, Bruce ordered champagne to toast Alex's future as a journalist. She protested, laughing, at his extravagant prophecies.

"I'm not that ambitious. It will never be of prime importance to me. Just an extension of my liking for natural history, that's all. I have thought that some day, perhaps, I'd write a book about the animal life and bird life of our river at Camerino."

"Your river?"

"Well, part of it is our boundary. My sister-in-law is very clever at drawing birds and animals, and I'd like her to illustrate it, if ever she gets free of babies. You'll like Sarah. She and Clive will be there on Sunday."

"I'm terribly sorry, Alex, but I shan't be able to come on Sunday, after all. Mother's giving a welcome home party to Eve Dalloway, and I'll have to be there. Didn't Mother tell you about it? She was full of it when I got home."

"Yes. I didn't think . . ."

"But I'll come some other time, my dear. Now, what about a crêpe suzette?"

She fought down her disappointment and the evening went along happily enough. During the next few days, she was kept busy helping Mrs Raynham to organise the party. Parties were the breath of life to her employer, but to Beth, who shouldered the donkey work, they must have been something of a burden, thought Alex as she listened to Mrs Raynham and Beth discussing the supper menu one morning.

"I think we'll have hors-d'œuvre to start with. They make the table look so pretty," said Mrs Raynham, tapping her chin with a pencil. "Then poultry, I suppose. A ham, too."

"How many are coming, then, Mother?"

"Oh, as many as I can muster. So far, I've about a dozen, but I shall be making a few more 'phone calls today. I'll give you the exact number tonight, dear. Is there anybody you'd particularly like?"

"No, Mother. I leave it to you."

"All right, dear. You must wear that midnight blue dress I bought for you. It suits you beautifully."

Beth smiled and left them.

"I'm so glad Beth's quite got over that dreadful Marksman boy. Did you hear that he was engaged to the greengrocer's daughter?"

"No."

"Well, that's what the chemist told me yesterday when I went in for some bath salts. He should know. He's right next door. But not a word to Beth. Best ignore it. I'm sure she's forgotten that foolish episode now, though. She's such a sensible person, really. That was just a . . ." She sought for the word, gesticulating with her beautiful bejewelled hand, and finally came out with "a mirage."

"She's seemed very quiet since that affair," said Alex.

"Oh, but Beth's always been a quiet girl. The excitement she displayed over Harry Marksman was quite foreign to her real nature. A kind of fever. Poor dear. It was so sad for her. But I've tried to make up for it since, and I told Juliet and Bruce to be specially nice to her. She's quite her happy, contented self again now, I know. She's coming to London with me next week to see Juliet's new home. You must come too, dear. It's really delightful."

"Thank you. I'd like to see it."

"Now, where was I? Ah, yes. Just take a note of the flowers I want ordered. We'll have red tulips, daffodils and irises. Oh, and I must have some freesias. Such heavenly flowers. And some palm. Now how many of each shall we want?"

When that was worked out, Mrs Raynham turned her attention to the wines and spirits. In the end, there was no time left before lunch for other work.

"Too bad you won't be here for the party, Alex. I suppose you must go home this week-end?"

"I promised."

"Well, never mind. You'll have plenty of opportunities to meet dear Eve. We shall be seeing a lot of her, I expect."

In fact, Alex met Eve Dalloway on the following Friday, when she went riding with Bruce and found that Eve was coming with them. When Bruce introduced them, he said,

"My mother's secretary is quite handy on a horse, Eve. You'll have to look to your laurels."

Eve ignored this, and held out her hand with a smile.

"I've heard a lot about you, Alex. I'm so glad to meet you."

She was a tall, slim young woman, with black hair neatly tucked away beneath her riding cap, regular features, a creamy complexion and dark grey eyes beneath delicately arched black brows. She looked very trim in her well-cut riding jacket and breeches and black boots, so that Alex, in jodhpurs and a sweater, bare-headed, felt something of a ragamuffin.

Alex was on Herod, and Eve rode the grey colt, Mercury, and Alex learned for the first time that the colt was hers, and that Bruce stabled and looked after it for her. Bruce had never allowed Alex to try Mercury, in spite of repeated requests, and they had not gone far before she realised that the colt might have proved too much of a handful for her, although Eve handled him superbly. They were all very friendly together; Eve told Alex about her world tour and promised to show her some coloured films, then drew her out about her work for Mrs Raynham. By the time they parted, Alex felt happily reassured about the nature of this latest addition to the Raynham circle.

On Saturday morning, Nigel offered to drive Alex home, as he passed very close to Camerino on his way to the building site, where he was meeting his architect and builder. It was a mild, sunny April day, with a blue sky and puffy white clouds sailing across it in a breeze which Alex declared smelt of primroses. The first shimmer of green showed on the hedges, and the blackthorn was in full bloom as they drove through the lanes.

"I love April," said Alex extravagantly. "The gateway to summer, with everything so fresh and bursting with life. I wish Bruce could have seen Camerino for the first time tomorrow. It looks its best now, with the Japanese cherries in bloom."

"Has he cried off tomorrow, then?"

"Yes. He couldn't very well come with this party planned for tomorrow."

"Why not today, then?"

"He's always too busy at the stables on Saturdays."

He gave a non-committal grunt and they were silent for several minutes until Nigel said carefully,

"I think you must be prepared to see less of Bruce now that Eve's home."

"Well, of course I don't expect to monopolise him."

"Just how serious are things between you two, babe?"

"We love each other. You don't think we'd go on as we do if we weren't in love, do you?"

"Bruce might," he said deliberately, and Alex felt her throat tighten and an angry little pulse started to make itself felt in that region.

"How dare you say that! I won't listen to your poisonous tongue, Nigel."

"I'm only trying to save you from getting hurt, but I suppose it's too late for that."

"You try to spoil everything. You suspect the motives of all the family, and a kinder, nicer lot of people I've never met. Now you're trying to poison my mind against Eve. The fact that she and Bruce have known each other all their lives and are good friends has nothing to do with how Bruce feels about me. We knew immediately we met. Bruce has never tried to hide it. To suggest that he's just amusing himself is vile. Why are you stopping?"

"Because I don't like driving through an argument." He drew up under the hedge and took out his cigarettes. "Don't think I particularly like this job, babe, but someone has to warn you. As long as I can remember, Bruce has had a young woman in tow. He likes women. No harm in it. Just his idea of good fun. Eve's always been there, though. Sometimes in the background, sometimes not. The year before her father died, there was nobody else but Eve."

"How do you know all this, since you lived in London and saw as little of the family as possible?" asked Alex coldly.

"Mother kept me in touch. She's very fond of the telephone, and no mean correspondent, either, as you've probably noticed. And Bruce and I have always got on all right. He's not a secretive chap. It's just that you don't understand them, Alex. They're not your sort, and you haven't a clue," he concluded despairingly.

"Then leave me to learn in my own way."

"All right. You've asked for it, and you shall be left to learn it. I'll make one prophecy, though. There's only one person Bruce will ever buy a wedding-ring for, and that's not you, babe."

"How very complimentary you are to me!"

"I am, as a matter of fact, but you won't see it. I'm trying to tell you that you're a person of integrity. The Raynhams just don't allow that uncomfortable word to filter into their minds. That's what puts a gap miles wide between you. They always find good reasons for believing what they want to believe to suit their own comfort, for acting as they want to act for their own ends."

"Why Eve and not me, then?"

"She has inherited just on a million for one thing," said Nigel coolly.

"You're contemptible. After this, I shan't have anything more to do with you. Please drive on and drop me off at Elton. I'll get a taxi from there."

"Right," said Nigel shortly. "You're a silly, head-in-the-clouds girl, and I give up. People like you shouldn't be let loose without a bodyguard. Why I should worry if you get hit over the head, I don't know."

They exchanged no more words until he stopped at Elton Station, when she gave him a frigid "Thank you". Then he astonished her again with one of those sudden twists of front which made him as difficult to handle as an eel. Putting a hand on her arm to detain her as she turned to get out, he gave her an odd little smile and said,

"I wanted to help you to grow up, Alex. It was foolish of me. Only experience can do that. Although you always see me with the devil's horns, believe me, this time my intentions were good."

"That's very hard to believe," said Alex severely.

"Just try," he said, amused by the struggle in her face.

He watched her cross the road, suitcase in hand, a slender figure in a pale green tweed suit and a matching beret stuck on at a rakish angle over the red-gold hair. She moved lightly, then suddenly kicked up her heels like a young colt as she ran forward waving to a taxi which was about to turn a corner. Nigel smiled to himself as she dived into the taxi, then he gave a little sigh as he put the Jaguar into gear and moved off. He had plenty of problems to think about with his new house. The sooner he dropped this father-protector attitude to young Alex, the better.

Chapter Eight

BACK in the secure atmosphere of her home, Alex felt the poison of Nigel's observations drain away, and she decided once again to have nothing more to do with him. He was dangerous. Her faith and pleasure in the Raynhams could be undermined by such tunnelling if she allowed the odd kind of friendship which had evolved between her and Nigel to go on. He was clever. When he saw that he had gone too far, he turned on the charm. She was ashamed that she had allowed any small doubts to creep in about the Raynhams because of his insinuations. She had always been staunch in her loyalties. With this last and most contemptible allegation that Bruce was merely playing with her, he had finally severed their friendship. She would listen to him no longer.

This resolve made, she felt compelled, as an act of faith, to tell her family more about Bruce than she had revealed before.

"It was too bad that he couldn't come, but this party was very awkward to duck," she said, when they were all gathered round the fire at tea-time on Sunday.

"Well, you know he'll be welcome any week-end with you, darling," said Mrs Madison, holding a plate of cakes for her grandson's inspection. David Madison, at six, found the choice an agonising one until his father told him to hurry up, whereat he seized a meringue.

"I'm curious to see this male wonder who has changed your ideas so rapidly, Alex," said Clive, watching with a critical eye the way his son tackled the meringue.

"He runs a riding school, didn't you say, Alex?" said Sarah hastily.

"Yes. He's a fine rider. He's won several cups for show jumping, too. Not that he's in the least conceited. Friendly and easy as you like. But they're all like that, the Raynhams. Friendly, and the greatest fun, and all most decorative. All except Beth, that is. It's a bit hard on her. Mrs Raynham and Juliet and Bruce have such exceptional good looks, and Beth was left out, but she's awfully nice."

"I didn't think so much of Mrs Raynham's appearance myself," said Clive. "At the wedding, I thought she looked too artificial. And all that silly chatter!"

"Very good-looking, I thought," said Sarah. "If Bruce is like her, he must be a stunner."

"He is. A real Apollo," said Alex. "Fair hair, blue eyes, the lot. But very masculine."

"It's what's underneath that matters, my girl," said her father.

"Oh, it's very good underneath," said Alex wickedly. "Just like Mother's Christmas cake under the icing."

"Well, you'd better bring him along and give us a taste, then," said Clive. "David has found a meringue something of a disappointment, I fancy. Pick up those pieces, young man, and try something less exotic."

David, who had inherited his father's dark grey eyes and square chin, and his mother's slow, sweet smile which he used with devastating effect, carefully picked up the pieces of sugar from his chair and the table, placed them in a neat pile in the centre of his plate, and took a piece of undeceptive fruit cake.

Outside, the spring sunshine lit up the fresh green of the garden, gay now with wallflowers and forget-me-nots and aubrietia. The pink blossoms of the Japanese cherry tree had dropped some of its petals to the lawn already. If only spring would stand still, thought Alex, as she watched a petal drift down and settle on the pram in which the baby, Elizabeth, slept peacefully. The sunshine and brilliant colour outside dimmed the fire within, and beckoned her out. If Bruce had been there, she could have taken him round the garden, shown him the river. It would probably be wet when he did come. She longed to show him Camerino in its sunny spring dress. It was such a perfect day to share with someone you loved.

They sat on, chatting idly round the fire. A reliable family, thought Alex, eyeing them with a new objectivity now that she lived away from them and her life had a different direction. As reliable as the old house itself. The portrait of her grandmother looked down at them above the fireplace. A pity she hadn't lived to see the youngest Madison, named after her, who was sleeping now in the spring sunshine. A pity, too, that Grandma Madison had not lived to see Bruce. She had an eye for a personable young man. When she was young, she had made the sparks fly round several young men, as her memoirs revealed if you read between the wryly discreet lines.

Alex accepted another cup of tea, and settled down lazily in her arm-chair, basking in a sense of happy security, dwelling with pleasure on her future with Bruce. How abominable Nigel's mind was! Bruce was as deeply in love with her as she with him. He had sought her out from the first, and his ardour had grown with hers. She had been right in her quip about needing a long spoon to sup with the devil. No spoon would be long enough to keep Nigel off.

She returned to Pelham House on Monday morning to find them all a little jaded after the party. She met Bruce in the drive, dressed for riding, and he gave her a friendly hug which warmed her heart.

"Just going to shake my liver up. A bit of a hangover this morning. We didn't break up until after two."

"Did you enjoy yourselves?"

"Rather. Went with a bang. Mother had invited some gay pals of hers. Only hope they all got home safely. Some of Eve's friends went back to sleep at The Grange. You look as fresh as a new coin, pet. Put down that suitcase and walk to the stables with me. Mother won't be making an early start today, I assure you."

She tucked her hand under his arm and told him about her week-end, and learned bits and pieces about the previous night's festivities at Pelham House. When they reached the stables, he drew her inside the entrance and kissed her.

"That's better," he said, as he raised his head. "I begin to feel myself. You're a nice kid, Alex. Do you know? A very . . . nice . . . kid." He punctuated the words with kisses, then let her go.

"You're not bad, either," she said, smiling.

"Now be off with you, instead of tempting me to linger. I've a young filly to school over the jumps this morning."

"I wish I was your assistant."

"That would be fatal. We'd never get any work done. Away to your typewriter, Delilah, and leave me to my filly. She's as pretty as you, and as frisky, but I don't somehow think she'll be as good a pupil."

She walked down the lane in a cloud of happiness. Nothing wrong there. In the hall, she met Beth, who looked tired to death, and when asked if she had enjoyed the party, merely said, "It was very noisy and went on too long, but I think they all had a good time," as though she did not come into it. Juliet, appearing in a housecoat while Alex was unpacking, announced that her mother was spending the morning in bed, but would be glad if Alex would get on with the article she had left on her desk.

"Heavens, what a party!" said Juliet, flopping down on Alex's divan. "I feel like a stale egg."

"Well, you don't look like one," said Alex, smiling at Juliet's pretty, fair face, its apple-blossom complexion and blue eyes quite undimmed by the previous night's activities. In her rose-sprigged housecoat and pink velvet slippers, she looked as fresh as a May morning.

"Thank goodness I haven't any classes today. I'll see if a cup of black coffee will restore me. Champagne never did suit me. Still, it was a grand party. Wish you'd been there, Alex. Did you have a nice week-end?"

"Yes, thanks. Fairly quiet. Just the family, including nephew and niece, who were both angelic, for a change."

Juliet drifted off, and Alex went to her office and began to type Mrs Raynham's article. She had nearly finished it when Mrs Raynham came in and greeted Alex with her usual gay smile.

"Isn't this a disgraceful time to start? But I felt I needed re-charging after last night. Such a lovely party, dear! I do wish you had been there. I never like the anti-climax afterwards, though."

"I'm not very good at parties," confessed Alex, "and secretly, I'm often relieved when they're over. That's when my spirits rise again."

"Then you've never been to the right parties, dear. At your age, you should revel in them. I do still, and I hope the day will never come when I'm too old to enjoy them."

"I'm sure it won't."

"I dread getting old and losing my vitality. I can't live without lots of people and life around me. I just wilt."

It was odd, thought Alex, to be so dependent on other people. Not to be able to bear being alone with oneself. For such people, life must always be a battle to keep solitude at bay. A battle that would tend to become more desperate with the years.

"Eve was in splendid form," went on Mrs Raynham.

"Travelling has improved her poise. It's so nice to have her back with us again. We've all missed her, especially Bruce, I fancy. The extravagant boy gave her such a pretty necklace for a welcome home present. Jade. She wore it last night with a black and jade dress. Really chic. She has style, that girl."

While Mrs Raynham chatted on about the party, Alex stifled the small demon of doubt that stirred. She had fought that battle with Nigel in the car. What sort of a person was she if her trust shook at every little knock?

She arranged with Bruce to have Herod for an hour the following evening, after work, and as she walked to the stables, the beauty of that spring evening filled her with its own confident promise. There were wild violets under the hedge, and a cherry tree in full bloom leaned over the lane with an ethereal, pearly sheen on its blossom in the light of the sinking sun. The air smelt sweet and fresh, and she traced the faint fragrance to a cluster of primroses in a field behind the hedge, and decided to pick a bunch for her room on her way back. She would suggest to Bruce that they went over the heath that evening. It was always especially beautiful in the evening light, with its silver birch trees and gorse bushes, seldom without flower, and the little paths of silvery sand which wound among the heather. And you could watch the sun sink down to the horizon of that flat expanse, changing all the colours of the heath as it sank.

Jackie greeted her with a smile, and led Herod out.

"Is Mr Raynham not coming?" asked Alex, surprised at his absence, for she had taken it for granted that they would ride together, as usual.

"He's out with Miss Dalloway, but he'll be back soon, because he's leaving early tonight. How long are you having Herod, Miss Madison?"

"I'll be back by half-past six," promised Alex, gathering the reins as she moved off.

She was the only person on the heath that evening, and she found that its beauty held melancholy, too. She went no faster than a walk for most of the way, letting the peace of the evening sink into her, keeping everything but the serenity of the evening at bay. She stopped by a silver birch tree to watch the red ball of the sun sink below the purple horizon, leaving a sky streaked with red and green and purple. Then she shook Herod into a canter, to which he responded eagerly, for he was headed for home.

It was nearly dark when she walked back along the lane and climbed a gate into the field where the primroses grew in clusters as pale as the moon. The light lasted just long enough for her to pick a bunch as large as her fist. The grass was wet with dew as she walked to the gate, and whether it was her wet shoes or the fact that one hand was occupied with the primroses, she did not know, but in climbing the gate, she fell inelegantly on the other side, still clutching her primroses intact while she shot out her free hand to save herself and ran a thorn into her thumb while doing so. She was picking herself up when the car stopped. It was Nigel on the way home.

"Hullo, there. Have you hurt yourself?"

She blinked in the lights of the car as she pulled her sweater down, and remembered that this was the man she had cut out of her life.

"I'm quite all right, thanks."

"Hop in, then."

"No, I'd rather walk. Thanks all the same."

"Quite sure?"

"Yes, thanks. It's only a few steps."

He had got out and now loomed over her. She held her damaged hand behind her.

"You went a real purler. Just picked you up in the lights at the crucial moment. Let's have a look at that hand."

He drew her closer to the side light and Alex studied the hand with some interest herself, uncertain what it was that was making it hurt so much. It was bleeding from a tear across the fleshy part of her thumb, deeply embedded in which was a wicked looking thorn, purple beneath the flesh, black where it protruded just above the surface.

"That won't be easy to get out intact," said Nigel. "You'd

better come back to the lodge with me and let me have a go. You'll never do it left-handed without making a horrible mess of it."

"Don't fuss, Nigel. Beth will give me a hand if I can't get it out myself."

She turned to walk off, but he caught her shoulder.

"You sound unusually chilly. Still angry with me for what I said about Bruce?"

"For what you say about all of them. I don't want to have my mind poisoned."

"You don't have to believe it. I do declare you're scared of me, Alex. I've never seen you look like this before."

And standing there beside the car with him, she did feel scared. He threatened her happiness. Everything he said carried weight with her, despite her protests. He was that sort of man. Dangerous.

"I don't want to have anything more to do with you, Nigel. I feel that you're a dangerous influence. Good night."

She slid out of his grasp and ran on up the lane. She was still running when she came to Pelham House, running as though the devil pursued her. The house was in darkness. A note on the hall table from Beth informed her that she had a headache and was so tired that she had gone to bed, leaving Alex's dinner in the dining-room. It also informed her that Mrs Raynham and Juliet had driven off to a cinema, Bruce was spending the evening at The Grange and Mr Raynham was not expected home. In the bathroom, Alex tried to deal with the thorn in her thumb, but she was clumsy with her left hand, and only succeeded in breaking off the small piece of thorn that had protruded. It was very painful, and as she washed it, she half wished that she had accepted Nigel's offer of help. She was dabbing Dettol on it when Nigel's voice came up the stairs.

"Alex."

She went out on to the landing and leaned over the stairs.

"Yes, what is it?"

"Ben told me that there was nobody at home here tonight. He came up ten minutes ago and left a parcel in the kitchen for Beth. Something she'd asked him to fetch from the cleaners."

"Sh. Beth's gone to bed with a headache."

"Well, don't hover there like Juliet on the balcony. Have you tackled that hand yet?"

"I'm just doing it."

"Want any help? If you don't get that thorn out, it may fester."

She hesitated and he came up the stairs and propelled her back into the bathroom. Under the light, he had a good look at it, then said,

"Shall I do it, or shall I run you down to the doctor's surgery?"

"I hate going to the doctor's. Surgeries depress me."

"And you hate turning to me. Which is the lesser of the evils?" he asked with his crooked smile.

She stuck out her hand.

"Have a go, and don't expect me to be a stoic. I expect I shall yell."

"That won't put me off, but it may disturb Beth, who will go into a flap, so I suggest we adjourn to the lodge where I have more efficient tools than that battered pair of tweezers."

"It surely doesn't call for a surgeon's kit," said Alex a shade apprehensively.

He grinned and put an arm round her shoulder as he said,

"Worse than that. Gouges specially made for the devil. As a matter of fact, Ben keeps a very excellent first-aid kit, being of a morbid disposition. Come on. Don't make a fuss. Afterwards, you can stay and have a really decent dinner with me instead of sitting down on your own to that depressing cold ham and beetroot."

In spite of her half-hearted protests, she somehow found herself in the bathroom of the lodge being operated upon by Nigel, a nasty looking row of implements laid out on the window-sill beside him. He took no notice of her wincing, apart from admonishing her to keep still, and was cool, ruthless and effective. When he had it out, she felt a little sick, but by the time he had put a small dressing on it, she had recovered.

"Good girl. That was a real brute. Now I'll get you a sherry, which we must down in a few minutes, or Ben will begin bleating about his dinner spoiling."

"I don't think . . ." Her voice trailed away as she met his eyes.

"You really would prefer cold ham on your own? I don't want to force you, of course, but Ben's roast duck smells delicious, and that's an awfully big dining-room in Pelham House for one young woman with nothing but a sore thumb and her dignity for company."

She looked at him helplessly, feeling her resolve slipping, and he waited, smiling. Why, thought Alex despairingly, could she not be firmer? She had never considered herself a wobbly character, but now both the resolutions so firmly taken at the week-end were slipping already. She looked down at her jodhpurs, feebly seeking a straw to save her.

"I'm not dressed for dinner."

"I'll bear with that. You look clean and tidy. That's all that matters. Now, which is it to be? Roast duck, green peas and new potatoes with the devil, or cold ham and beetroot on your own?"

It was no use, she thought. She couldn't make an enemy of him, still less could she ignore him.

"I'll settle for the duck," she said with a little smile, "and send up a prayer for my immortal soul. I'm terribly hungry."

The dinner was delicious, and sitting by the fire in the sitting-room afterwards, with Nigel presiding over the coffee-pot, she wondered whether Bruce had enjoyed such a good dinner at The Grange with Eve and her mother.

"I'm going to send you packing after this," said Nigel, with the good-humoured candour with which he always treated her. "I've some work to do, and you've got your immortal soul to think of."

"I expect you think I'm very foolish. I am, too. I've never felt so confused in my mind before."

"I don't think you're foolish. Only inexperienced."

"Must you be inexperienced if you trust people and believe in their goodness?" she said with a desperation that sent Nigel's eyebrows up. It always annoyed her, this capacity of his for detachment, and she went on quickly, before he could give her a cool answer. "It's you who sow all the seeds of doubt in my mind. And yet, I don't believe that you're a malicious person. In fact, I know you're not. Have you been let down badly by somebody at some time in your life, Nigel? Someone you trusted? Has that made you so sceptical about people's motives and behaviour?"

Nigel choked over his coffee at the sudden look of concern in her face. When he had recovered, he said, with laughter in his voice,

"Dear babe, it's kind of you to try to find excuses for my jaundiced nature, but I'm afraid I can't even plead that romantic excuse for my evil mind. I've got from people more or less what I expected."

"Then the world must be a very black place to you," said Alex tartly, annoyed that he should laugh at her.

"On the contrary. I enjoy life, and I find the world an interesting and amusing place, now that I've learned not to take people too seriously. You're so intense, babe. So carried away with your feelings that you forget to take a cool, deep look at people."

"I don't put them on a slab under my microscope, like you. But what's the use of arguing? I won't let you poison my mind against Bruce and the others. Unless you promise me to stop, I'd rather have nothing more to do with you."

"I told you on Saturday that I'm leaving you to learn your lesson now. I've tried to warn you only for your own sake. I never have agreed with interfering in other people's affairs, and it was foolish to break my own rules, but I like you, babe, and it really did seem a case of an innocent in the jaws of the Raynham crocodile. However, what I said on Saturday holds. The field is all yours. But don't ask me to butter up the truth as I see it to spare your ideals. I'll refrain from further comment about Bruce, since that is what has really upset you, but don't look for cosy half-truths between us, Alex. I'm not made that way. Nor, I fancy, for all your romantic illusions, are you. Now, do you want to be ignored by this particular devil, or not? It's up to you."

What could she believe? Was he a friend trying to warn her, or a cold-hearted cynic who took pleasure in undermining other people's faith? She thought of Bruce's open, laughing face, which had brought so much enjoyment into her life, and looked at the dark, slightly mocking face opposite her which had brought so much discomfort. And yet, she knew that Nigel's respect for truth was genuine, that he carried it into his personal life as well as his work. But truth about people was never final. The truth as he saw it could be wrong. Must be wrong. In the end, she heard herself saying, almost in spite of herself, as she stood up to go,

"Not ignored. But walk round my dreams, Nigel."

"Have I been such a brute?" he asked, smiling gently.

"No, not really," she said, looking at the dressing on her thumb. "No. In many ways, you've been very kind. That's what makes you so puzzling. I feel your kindness, and I hear your cruel tongue. But, of course, it would be much worse if it were the other way round. Thank you, Nigel, for the kindness," she concluded, veering now to the feeling that she had been unfair to him.

"Say no more. On that friendly note, we will close the discussion," he declared solemnly, putting a hand on her shoulder for a moment as he walked to the door with her.

She was as unstable as a seesaw, she thought unhappily as she went up the drive. First up in the air, shining with love and faith in Bruce, then down with a bump when Eve's name was mentioned. Up in the air again, convinced that Nigel was responsible for her lack of confidence; down again, recognising his regard for truth. At one moment, sure that she had driven out his evil influence, at the next, comforted in some queer way because he had not been cast out. What was the matter with her, that she could no longer think straight? Was this what being in love did to you? Reduced your mind to a wobbling jelly. If only Bruce had been there on that mild spring night to take her in his arms and chase all fears away.

Chapter Nine

"Is anything the matter, Alex dear? You've not seemed your usual bright self this past week or two," observed Mrs Raynham.

"No, I'm quite all right, thank you," said Alex, her pencil poised over her notebook, for they were in the middle of their correspondence.

"I think perhaps you need a little holiday. I'm working you too hard."

"No. Really, there's nothing to bother about."

"But I do bother. We're all so fond of you. I bother as much as if you were my own child, and I know Bruce looks on you as a sister. You miss him a little, perhaps, now that Eve's come home. I know I do. The boy's hardly ever home, it seems."

Alex studied the last outline in her book as she said,

"He's certainly well occupied these days."

"If I were a match-making mother, I couldn't wish for a better choice for Bruce than Eve. But when two people have known each other for so long and nothing comes of it, you just assume it's friendship and no more. Bruce has such a friendly, easy-going nature, as you know."

"Yes."

"I suggest you come up to London with me tomorrow, Alex, and we'll go on a shopping spree and perhaps do a matinée. You need cheering up. All work and no play isn't good for young folk. Now not another word. We'll catch the ten-five train tomorrow morning."

"It's very kind of you, Mrs Raynham, but I must get my

own column written tomorrow," said Alex, who wondered if she was going to be given a blouse from Harrods, too.

"Oh, nonsense. You can polish that off today."

"Not with your London articles and these letters to do. And really, you know, I don't much like London."

"Not like London! Then you don't like life, dear," said Mrs Raynham gaily. "But I won't press you. Another time, perhaps. I want to see how the decorators are getting on at Juliet's house tomorrow, and it would be difficult perhaps to fit shopping and a theatre in as well. But I insist on your adding an extra day or two on to the next week-end you go home. You mustn't make me feel a tyrant. Those pale cheeks won't do."

Alex smiled and endeavoured to look healthy until she was alone again, when she sat back in her chair and gazed at her typewriter with a baffled look. How did one handle such a situation? When she saw Bruce, he was as friendly and affectionate as ever, but they were seldom alone and he was always too busy to go riding with her now. Should she ask him outright if he had changed towards her? By nature she was a downright person, but she shrank from the crudity of a frontal assault in such a matter. His attitude to Eve was difficult to assess. She didn't see them together often, for, if they met, it was away from home. But she would have staked her life on the sincerity of Bruce's love, and for all Mrs Raynham's allusions to fraternity, there had been nothing platonic about Bruce's attentions. Perhaps Mrs Raynham had been warning her. Putting on the label which would cause least trouble and enable everybody to be happy. She pushed a weary hand through her hair. She had been fighting a rearguard action against Nigel's insinuations for a month now, but the doubts were beginning to gain ground.

That evening, she persuaded Beth to come to her room to listen to some records. She had discovered that Beth shared her taste in music, and she seemed to enjoy spending an hour or two in Alex's room, although she always needed a lot of persuading, since she could never apparently believe that Alex really wanted her. That evening was no exception, and she hovered at the door uncertainly.

"Are you sure I shan't be in the way, Alex? You must need to get away from us all sometimes."

"I'm quite sure, Beth. I like you to share the music with me. I enjoy it more if you're there. Pleasures shared are doubled."

"Really? That *is* kind of you."

"You know, you shouldn't think so little of yourself. I wish you'd come out walking with me sometimes. You go out so seldom, and you see so few people, except for the parties here, and then you're so busy that you don't have time to enjoy them."

"I prefer to be busy. I'm not good at mixing with people. In fact, I'm always half scared at these parties of Mother's, but for heaven's sake don't tell her, or she'd think I was mad. She doesn't understand what it's like to be plain and shy. She's so different. She's quite marvellous, of course. I sometimes wonder how she ever came to have a daughter like me. Juliet and Bruce, now, are the logical outcome."

"People are individuals. Not just liked for charm and looks. It's what's inside that matters, as my father is always saying."

"I used to try to believe that once, but not now. I made a fool of myself by letting myself think it. Never again."

Beth's face was flushed and tense as she sat on the edge of her chair. It was a cold night for May, and Alex made her draw the chair up to the electric fire, and gave her a cushion for her back while she busied herself with the records.

"We all get let down by people sometimes," she said gently.

"That's not the same thing."

"I asked for it. The humiliation was so awful that I could have killed myself that night."

"Oh, Beth! It could have happened to anybody." She could have added that it was probably happening to her at that very moment.

"Not in that way. But let's not talk about it. It taught me a lesson. What shall we have?"

"Swan Lake ballet?"

"Lovely."

They listened in silence, Beth leaning back, relaxed now, her eyes half closed, while Alex sat on a cushion on the floor and leaned against the window seat on which was the portable gramophone. It was not a very good one, as had been made all too evident to her when she had heard Nigel's record player, and she intended to save up for a better one, but it still afforded her a good deal of enjoyment. That evening, however, the music did not hold her, and her thoughts wandered. It occurred to her for the first time that Beth must have been treated with some insensitivity by her family to have harboured such an intense inferiority complex into years of maturity. It was a little hard to be surrounded by such a battery of charm as the Raynhams possessed, but there were other values. These, she realised, were not the kind that were emphasised in Pelham House. Was Nigel right, then? Was all this frothy charm all there was? Was it just a convenient cloak for materialistic lives? She remembered feeling that her own family was dull by comparison with the Raynhams. Now she would have given much for the sense of security they had always engendered. And much, too, for her grandmother's pithy counsel. What would she advise now? A frontal attack, probably, asking Bruce just what game he was playing, for Grandmother Madison had been a spirited old lady, with plenty of pride. But Alex was young and in love for the first time. She believed in Bruce's good faith, but she hesitated to challenge it. There seemed to be no alternative to letting time give the answer, but the inactivity chafed her.

After the music, Beth went to fetch a tray of tea, and returned with Bella panting at her heels.

"She would follow me, Alex. Do you mind?"

"Of course not. She has a habit of sneaking up here, especially if I'm not around at walking times."

Bella flopped down on the hearthrug, and rested her old grey muzzle on Alex's foot.

"I don't know about you, but I'm getting a little tired of all this fuss about Juliet's wedding," said Beth, putting the tray on the little coffee table between them. "I suppose that sounds catty, and a case of sour grapes, but Juliet does so little herself and expects everybody else to run themselves to a standstill. I've got miles of net curtains to machine for her."

"I thought all the curtains were being made by the firm of interior decorators your mother found."

"Not the nets. They thought I could do those. Oh, it's beastly of me to quibble. Sometimes it frightens me, the sour way I think these days. Forget it, Alex. I'm just getting crabby."

"No, you're not. Everybody takes advantage of your willing nature. I think Juliet ought to do more, but I suppose she's always been spoilt, and Barney will carry on with it, too. He's awfully nice, isn't he?"

"Yes. I sometimes wonder if Juliet cares much for him. She treats him like a little boy. A pat on the head, a sweet smile and perhaps half an hour of her time to keep him happy. Oh, dear! There I go again. And I've enjoyed this evening so much. Let's change the subject to something safe."

Alex smiled and led her on to her plans for the garden, of which Beth was very fond. It was true, she thought, that a little strain of bitterness crept into Beth's quiet voice sometimes now, and Alex's heart ached for her. The years were damaging her with their denial of the fulfilments which most young people took for granted. She had little freedom, no companionship, and a hard-working, monotonous life. The fact that it was her own lack of confidence in herself which did more than anything to put prison bars around her made it no less sad.

Bella let out a tremendous sigh, as though life was too much for her, and Alex's eyes suddenly danced with amusement. Here they were: Beth frustrated and unhappy, Alex deserted by her lover, and the dog old and mournful. It was like a Chekhov play.

"Come out with Bella and me tonight, Beth. We find all sorts of exciting things, and there's nothing like a little nature study to stop you thinking about your troubles."

"All right. But no snakes, I hope. I'm not so fond as you are of things that crawl."

The next evening Alex was alone in her room putting the finishing touches to her article when there was a knock at her door and Juliet's head appeared.

"Alex, Mother says you simply must come down. We've some excitement in the drawing-room."

"Just a few minutes," said Alex, her brows furrowed. The last paragraph was weak, somehow.

"O.K. But don't be long."

Alex was not unduly curious about the excitement, for scarcely a day passed without Mrs Raynham making a pronouncement of exciting news, or having something to show them. After a day in London, it might mean no more than a "find" for Juliet's home. Last time, it had been a very beautiful antique brooch which Mrs Raynham had bought for herself at a price which had made her husband blench.

Alex leaned back and wondered whether she ought to re-type the article. It looked a bit messy with so many alterations. In the end, she decided to go into the office before breakfast the next morning and type it again. If she left it until later, it would probably get crowded out by Mrs Raynham's work, which was usually heavy after a day in London, and she had promised to drop her article into Mr Barling's office before it closed the next day.

She went downstairs, still preoccupied with her article, to find the whole family, including Nigel, assembled in the drawing-room with Eve Dalloway and an elderly woman unknown to Alex. Her eyes went first, as always, to Bruce. He had not been in to dinner, and must have just returned with Eve. He smiled vaguely and looked away.

"Come and meet Eve's mother, Alex dear, and then we'll drink our toast. Leonard, pour some sherry for Alex. She prefers that," said Mrs Raynham, her face alight with excitement.

Alex shook hands with the tall, thin, white-haired lady, who seemed very composed. When Eve crossed the room and tucked her hand under Bruce's arm, Alex knew instantly, with a shock which seemed to run through her like a powerful current of electricty.

"Now, Leonard," said Mrs Raynham, turning to her husband.

Nigel moved in front of Alex as Mr Raynham said,

"We're all delighted at the news of Bruce's engagement to Eve. They've been long enough about it, but we'll forgive them that. After all, it's an important decision to take. For myself, I have no doubts that it's a very happy decision, and I am sure that we all feel the same. Our toast is, Eve and Bruce. May they reap great happiness."

It would have been easier for Alex if there had been more people there, so that her own congratulations might have been omitted unnoticed, but she managed to pin a smile to her face as she offered her congratulations with Nigel at her elbow. Then he had jostled her on and was adding a few urbane words of his own. It was a good thing that one never had to make a sustained effort at any social occasion when Barbara Raynham was present, thought Alex. She gathered most people's attention for most of the time, and that evening was no exception.

Alex had lost count of time when the gathering broke up, and Bruce drove Eve and her mother home. She could not have said what had passed since that toast, only found that it was nearly midnight when she murmured something about taking Bella down the lane.

"You can't go at this time, Alex dear," cried Mrs Raynham.

"Walk down to the lodge with me," said Nigel. "That'll give Bella the delusion that she's had her walk."

She nodded blindly and went to fetch the dog, conscious of only one wish. To get into the open air, away from everybody. Mrs Raynham was in the hall when she returned with Bella.

"Alex, my dear, all this excitement has quite made me forget the little present I brought back from London for you. The prettiest nylon nightie you ever did see. I'd have liked it for myself, but I thought it was more suitable, perhaps, for a young girl. You'll look ravishing in it. I simply must fetch it for you now."

"How kind of you, Mrs Raynham!" said Alex steadily, and wondered at her own calm. "I wonder if you would leave it in my room in case I'm longer with Bella than you expect. I shall go a little way down the lane. I've a headache, and I think the fresh air might blow it away."

"You and your fresh air, Alex. All right, my dear. It's all the excitement and the drink. I feel a little heady myself. I'll lay it out on your bed and you shall tell me tomorrow how you like it. It's that heavenly blue-green, the colour of Arden's blue grass hand lotion. It will look ravishing with your hair."

"We must get you to parade in it for our benefit, Alex," said Nigel, ushering her through the front door ahead of him as he turned to say good night to his mother.

When he caught her up by the gates, she turned to him, half laughing, half sobbing.

"Beth had a blouse," she gasped, "and I've got a nightie." Then the tears came and she walked on blindly, saying, "Please let me go on alone, Nigel."

"No."

He handed her a handkerchief, and walked beside her in silence as she tried to stem the tears. Gradually, the cold night air and the silence had their effect and she regained control of herself, although she could not stop trembling.

"I'm sorry," she said in a quavering voice. "It was the shock, and I had too much sherry, I think."

"Feel sick?"

"No. Only a bad head. Where's Bella?"

"Lord knows." He whistled and called impatiently.

"She can't hear voices any more," said Alex, gulping. "I have to clap my hands." She fumbled with her gloves and clapped her hands sharply, whereat Bella loomed up from a ditch and started walking in the opposite direction.

"What a dog!" said Nigel.

"She can't help it. She's nearly blind and she gets in a bit of a panic when she can't see you, which always seems to send her in the wrong direction."

"Here, give me the lead."

Nigel sprinted after Bella and put the lead on her.

"It seems to me this old dog's had it," said Nigel, when he rejoined her. "She's blind and silly."

"Not more than I am," said Alex bitterly.

"I'm sorry, babe."

"I know. Thank you. I can't talk about it."

"Righto. Ready to turn back?"

"Yes. I'll take Bella. She's not silly. She's very intelligent, and her nose tells her where she wants to go. She has a good two years or more in front of her, if she's looked after."

"What a soft heart you have! It's really far too soft for this world, you know."

But she could say no more, and their footsteps echoed in the lane as they walked back through the silent night. When they reached the lodge, Nigel put a hand on her shoulder and squeezed it as he said good night.

"Take some aspirins and try to sleep. I'd like to wring Bruce's neck, but that wouldn't do you any good."

"No," she said blankly, "it wouldn't. Good night, Nigel. Thank you for not saying I told you so."

He watched her plodding up the drive, the dog trailing at her heels. She usually walked so freely, with her head in the air, as though she really enjoyed it. He sighed and shrugged his shoulders, then went into the lodge.

Chapter Ten

WHEN Alex looked back on the affair, she realised how cleverly it had been stage managed to cause no embarrassment. Every member of the Raynham family, with the exception perhaps of Mr Raynham, who lived a life apart from his family, must have noticed the marked attentions Bruce had paid her from the time of her arrival, and the closeness of their friendship, but they all took their cue from Mrs Raynham in skating over any possibility of awkwardness, behaving as though Alex shared their pleasure at Bruce's engagement. As for Bruce himself, his strategy was superb. Without making it at all obvious, he saw to it that he was never alone with Alex, but in the presence of others he always treated her with jovial affection. If this sleight of hand came off successfully in the family circle, however, Eve Dalloway made it clear one evening a few weeks after their engagement that she had a pretty shrewd idea of what had been going on in her absence.

They were all at dinner when Bruce announced that he and Eve intended to be married in a register office in a fortnight's time, and he was at once subjected to a barrage of protests from Juliet and his mother. He laughed good-humouredly and held up his hand.

"Now, my dears. You'll have all the fun and games you need, all the dressing up and fuss in the world, at Juliet's wedding next month. Eve has just found a splendid country house with fifty acres of land which will be fine for breeding and training our own horses for show jumping and steeple-chasing. We want to get on with it, and Eve prefers a quiet wedding, anyway. After all, you'll have plenty of time to get a new hat from Harrods, darling," he said, with a teasing smile for his mother.

"Well, I'm disappointed. I do love a proper wedding. However, if you children have decided, I'll say no more. I do think it's a bit sudden, though."

"Not really, Mrs Raynham," said Eve. "Bruce has been awfully patient and waited for a long time, you know. He was very cross with me for wanting my year abroad before I'd finally give him my answer, but he agreed to wait. I don't think it would be fair to keep him waiting much longer, and it would take a lot of time to organise a big wedding. Time we don't want to spare."

"Well, bless you, I've always made it a rule to let my children make their own decisions, and very capable they are at it, too," said Barbara Raynham, smiling sweetly. She must have forgotten Beth, thought Alex, as the melodious voice went on. "And I must say that I think it was most sensible of you, Eve, to take that year abroad to see the world after you inherited your father's money. A splendid experience for a young girl. I'm glad, though, that no other young man tempted you while you were away."

"I wouldn't say that, Mrs Raynham," said Eve, her eyes sparkling as she looked across at Bruce. "But we made a bargain to give each other complete freedom in that respect for a year. I thought it would help me to decide whether Bruce was the one and only. After all, I'd met very few men while Daddy was alive. Bruce had always filled the horizon. I thought I'd like to see what the world could offer. And I admitted Bruce's right to experiment for that year, too."

"How wise you are for a young person, Eve!" said Mrs Raynham. "Most young people are so possessive with each other. Wide experience is so good for the character. It makes for tolerance and understanding."

"Yes. But the experimental stage is over now. We've had our fling. Now it's steady going, my boy," said Eve, smiling across the table at Bruce.

"I'm glad to hear it," he said.

Alex found Eve's grey eyes studying her coolly, and knew that she had been warned off. Knew, too, that Eve had steered the conversation deliberately to that end. Eve Dalloway was no fool.

Alex clenched her hands under the tablecloth and asked Beth to pass the bread. She found it hard to believe that anyone could be so calculating with a person they loved. Either you loved them and wanted nothing more than to be with them, or you didn't. This sampling of others to see if they tasted any better than your first choice seemed so cold and callous that she could not understand it. But then, she understood very little about people, it seemed. All her judgments were wrong. She felt lost and humiliated and desperately unhappy as she sat there with the lively conversation of the Raynhams going on around her. Like a coloured ball on a Christmas tree, Nigel had said. Played with until he had something better to do. Filling in the time until Eve should let him know her decision. And she had not recognised such intense involvement as play, and found such a concept so revolting that she shivered now as she thought of that night he had driven her home after the dance, of the postscripts to their evening walks with Bella, when, in the shadow of the lodge, he had so often taken her in his arms and time had ceased to be. Her cheeks burned at the recollection. Just a game. He would never know what he had done to her. She felt so ashamed that she could have wept if anger had not come to her aid and kept her sitting there at the dining-table, silent but betraying nothing. It was her first experience of duplicity, and it had both shocked and shattered her.

Gradually, however, as the weeks passed, her attitude hardened, and she came to regard the experience as a salutary lesson in the nature of men, whom she had always regarded with caution until Bruce appeared in her life and made a fool of her. She would know better another time. She was finished with men.

She confided this arbitrary decision to Nigel one Saturday morning when he was driving her over to see his house, and he chuckled.

"Is that meant as a warning to me, too?"

"Oh, you're different. You feel the same about women as I do about men, anyway."

"What makes you say that?"

"It's implicit in your whole attitude. Not that you seem to have a very high opinion of people at all, irrespective of sex."

"Dear me. I'd no idea you knew so much about my innermost feelings towards your sex."

"I don't. You're too well armoured to reveal much, but you stand aside and view all human beings with a mocking kind of detachment that shows you think very little of the human race, and that includes women."

"I don't let the human race harrow me, if that's what you mean. And I don't expect too much. I'm glad to see you've gathered up the pieces Bruce broke and stuck them together again, though."

"Nobody's going to make a fool of me again," said Alex fiercely. "It was horrible. So cynical, somehow."

And as she said it, it struck her as strange that Bruce, the friendly charming young man, should have dealt with her youth so cynically, while the cynical young man at her side would never have given her such counterfeit coin. He would be quite capable of amusing himself, but he would make it plain that amusement was the order of the day. Of the two, Nigel's biting tongue and cool detachment were less cruel than Bruce's kind tongue and warm affection. It was all very confusing.

Nigel glanced at her serious face, which was paler than usual and marked with dark shadows under her eyes. It hadn't been so easy to pick up the pieces, he surmised.

"Well, all lessons have to be paid for, my dear. I doubt, though, whether you're ever going to be the tough, man-proof character you think you are now. You can't keep your heart in a refrigerator. Wrong type."

"Tell me how to do it. You manage it all right. But then, you're a scientist, and for men it's different anyway."

"Are scientists all cold-blooded creatures, then?"

"Many are, I think. And you're scientific by nature as well as by profession. That's obvious. Have you ever thought you might want to marry?"

"Never," he said promptly.

"I thought not. You do seem to manage very comfortably without, I must say. Do you have any use for women at all?"

"Of course. I find them charming, when I'm in the mood for diversion," he said mischievously.

"But you wouldn't want them invading your life. You plan to live always as a bachelor in your house, with Ben to look after you and keep you comfortable without any petticoat trouble."

Nigel smiled as he drew up at the building site.

"Correct, but why this analysis of me?"

"I think you're very successful at living a satisfactory life, and I'd like to learn how to live alone and like it. I intend to make journalism and natural history my sole interest now, but I'd like a few hints from you about cutting people out, not getting involved. This episode with Bruce has shaken my confidence in myself. I think I must be a very foolish person. I don't get anybody right."

"The realisation of one's own foolishness is the beginning of wisdom, babe. And to confuse you more and confound your judgment of me as a man of no feeling, come and meet two people whose friendship does mean something to me. Quite a lot, in fact."

He led her through a litter of planks, drain pipes, tiles and scaffolding towards a tall, dark man in a tweed jacket and grey flannels, who was talking to the builder, gesticulating with his pipe towards the roof rafters. Beside him stood a girl with short chestnut hair wearing a honey-coloured tweed suit. She turned as she heard their footsteps and Alex saw a heart-shaped little face with large brown eyes, and a wide mouth which revealed slightly irregular teeth as she smiled delightedly.

"Guy, here's the master of the house. Hullo, Nigel. Nice to see you."

"My favourite girl. Bless you," said Nigel, kissing her cheek. "Morning, Guy. Bullying Downley as efficiently as usual?"

Nigel grinned at the builder, who shook his head, more in sorrow than in anger, and said patiently,

"If that's all, Mr Carstairs, I'll get the men to change that soffit now."

"Righto. Hullo, Nigel. It's shaping up all right, in spite of constant passive resistance from Downley. Don't think he approves of me," added Guy Carstairs reflectively as he watched the man disappear round the side of the half-built house.

"No builder ever approves of an architect," said Nigel. "Jane, allow me to introduce my mother's secretary, Miss Madison, otherwise Alex. Mr and Mrs Carstairs."

Jane Carstairs gave her a shy smile. Guy Carstairs was very impressive, thought Alex; tall and dark, with a Roman nose and a mouth with a jutting underlip which made him look formidable until he put an arm round his wife's shoulder and smiled down at her. She looked diminutive beside him.

"There you are, Jane. You've been wanting to meet her, and

now here she is. My wife's been throwing out hints to Nigel that she'd like to meet you ever since she picked up a magazine at his place and read your country article."

"I liked it so much," said Jane simply.

The two men went ahead, discussing building technicalities, while Jane conducted Alex through the downstairs rooms. They left the skeleton of the upstairs rooms to the two men, for the ascent looked a somewhat perilous business, but Alex could see enough to judge that the house would be most comfortable to live in, and when Jane showed her a coloured drawing of the finished house, she realised that it would be very elegant to look at. Trust Nigel, she thought, to have the best of all worlds. There was about an acre of ground containing many fine specimen trees, for Nigel's house had been built in what had been the garden of an old manor house, recently demolished. It could be turned into a beautiful garden, thought Alex, with that fine background of hills and beechwoods in the distance. Set back from the lane, the house was well screened from the few houses sparsely dotted about the neighbourhood.

"When will it be finished?" asked Alex.

"Later than we'd hoped. Probably not until August."

"I think it's going to be a delightful house. You have a very clever husband, Mrs Carstairs."

Jane smiled her thanks for this compliment and said,

"He's taken a special pride in this house. He and Nigel are very old friends, you know. I'm glad you didn't arrive ten minutes earlier. You'd have thought I was married to a terrible brute. He found that the builder had used asbestos where he should have used oak, for this soffit here," said Jane, pointing it out on the drawing, "and did Guy blow up! Vandalism, he called it. Come to the end of the garden with me. There's a nest of blackbirds in a cypress tree. Quite low down. Three of them, almost fledged."

When the men came in search of them half an hour later, they found them watching two baby hedgehogs foraging for food along the hedge.

"I might have known it," said Nigel. "Do you realise, Alex,

that the bus you intended to catch at the end of the lane left five minutes ago?"

"Oh, help!" said Alex. "I forgot the time. And it's an hourly service, isn't it?"

"Yes. I'll run you back to Camerino before going on to Jane's. Do you mind, Jane? It won't take me more than half an hour."

"That's all right, Nigel. It's cold lunch today, anyway. But won't you come to lunch, too, Alex?"

"I'd love to, but my family are expecting me home to lunch. Another time, if I may."

In the car with Nigel, Alex apologised for causing him the extra journey.

"That's all right. How did you like the house?"

"I thought it was lovely, that is, it will be lovely. A superb drawing-room, with those huge windows. Rather spacious for a bachelor, isn't it?"

"I like to entertain my friends without feeling cramped. Ben's had the last word over the kitchen, of course."

"It must be fun to have your own house built just as you want it, and watch it materialising."

"It is. I've got no end of a kick out of it. Guy's a good architect. He designed their own house a year or two ago, and that gave me one or two ideas."

"I like the Carstairs. How long have you known them, Nigel?"

"I've known Guy since my twenty-first birthday, and that was, let me see, twelve years ago. I met him at a hotel in Devon which his mother managed, and still does. I'd gone there to escape from the party my mother had threatened me with, and Guy was spending a week there. I found he was a good golfer. I'd just started, and he taught me a lot. We spent quite a pleasant few days together, I remember. Then I found that he was in rooms in London quite close to the flat I lived in, and that's how we got to know each other. A good chap."

"He works in London still, doesn't he?"

"Yes. Has his own practice. Offices in Westminster. Doing pretty well now. He used to have a taste for brassy young women, and when he told me he was engaged, I thought he'd sunk himself. Could have knocked me down with a feather when he introduced me to our little Jane. Just the opposite of his youthful girl friends."

"She's a delightful person. So simple and unaffected."

"I thought you'd like her. She's your type, in a way, but not so impetuous and effervescent. It's worked, anyway. They're very happy, and Guy wears his domestic chains as though they were made for him."

"I wonder how Bruce will wear his," said Alex with a little edge to her voice.

"Quite charmingly, I've no doubt. Did you find the wedding much of an ordeal? You looked unusually composed, if I may say so."

"I felt quite blank. Let's not talk about it."

"Righto. And now we have Juliet's wedding to face in a week's time. Upon my soul, all this matrimony is very boring."

His lazy drawl made Alex shoot a quick glance at him. He drove easily, relaxed behind the wheel, his eyes on the road ahead, presenting a lean, impenetrable profile which she suddenly found irritating. It was unfair to be so immune to the battering of personal relationships, and superhuman to be able to run one's life so competently to plan.

Walking up the drive to her home, Alex was aware of feeling tired, an experience so rare that she wondered if she was sickening for something. It would be a relief to relax at home for the week-end.

Chapter Eleven

JULIET's high, clear voice giving a telephone number floated clearly through the open door of the drawing-room where Alex, Beth and Mrs Raynham were drinking their after-dinner coffee. It was a warm evening, and they had opened the French doors on to the terrace.

"Is that you, Barney? You sound muffled, darling . . . Poor dear . . . Listen, Barney. I'm most terribly sorry, but would you mind not coming tonight? I've a most frightful headache, and I'm going to lie down . . . No, of course not . . . How sweet of you . . . Yes, darling, I'll ring you to-morrow . . . 'Bye."

Juliet came back into the drawing-room and picked up her cup of coffee. She looked very well indeed, as she always did, but Beth asked her if she would like some aspirins.

"No thanks, Beth. I'm quite all right, but I want to give myself a manicure and face treatment this evening."

"How can you want any treatment? You have a perfect skin," said Beth.

"Bless you, but I find it nice and relaxing lying on the bed with a face pack on. And there's always room for improvement."

It seemed to Alex an odd way of enjoying a summer evening, and to prefer it to seeing her fiancé was a strange comment on their relationship. There were only four days to go to their wedding, but Juliet showed no signs of excitement. She was her usual affable self, quick with her smiles and compliments. It occurred to Alex now as she looked at her pretty fair face that Juliet was like a meringue. If you bit into her, you'd find nothing but sugar and air.

"Poor Barney," said her mother with arch playfulness. "You are a little naughty with him, darling."

"I'm not. He's a pet, and I adore him, but I'm not in the mood for him tonight. Sometimes, he's a teeny weeny bit ponderous, bless him. Anyway, it's a long way for him to drive from London just for an hour or two with me tonight. He sounded a bit tired. He works terribly hard, poor sweet."

"You must look after him when you're married," said Beth in a dry little voice.

"Oh, I shall. Thank goodness we've been lucky in finding good domestic staff. I like that housekeeper you chose, Mummy. A real find."

"Yes. It's a little easier in London to find them. You're a lucky girl, you know, to have that lovely house in Hampstead, and no housekeeping worries."

"Yes. But what's the use of money if it can't make you comfortable? Barney will be away a lot, so you'll have to come and keep me company sometimes, Mummy. We can do theatres without having to worry about catching that last train home. We shall always have a room for you. And you might give me a hand at organising parties when Barney wants them. You're so good at it."

"I love them. I couldn't live without lots of people. And that reminds me. About the party coming on here after the reception, Alex. Will you order another case of wine? There will be more people coming than I expected and we don't want to run short."

* * *

The sun shone on Juliet's wedding day, and it seemed as though most of the village had turned out to see the loveliest bride Bridgefield had produced for years. It all went off beautifully, but to Alex, it seemed strangely unreal, like a film wedding.

Bruce, an usher, greeted Alex with a warm smile when she arrived at the church with Beth. Nigel, swooningly immaculate in morning dress, joined them in their pew only a minute before the bride arrived. Barney's portly figure, waiting at the altar, looked lonely and somehow pathetic. And then Juliet was played in, looking taller than usual in her white lace dress with its sweeping train. She carried a bouquet of pink and white roses, and wore a wreath of white rosebuds and lilies of the valley. Her father partnered her slender grace with handsome dignity. Behind her came two diminutive bridesmaids, dressed in high-waisted, Kate Greenaway dresses of pale blue silk with wreaths of forget-me-nots on their small, dark heads, and small baskets of the same flowers in their hands. They were only five years old, but they played their part with grave care and never faltered. They were Barney's twin nieces, and had obviously been well drilled.

It was all quite perfect, as any social function organised by Mrs Raynham would be, thought Alex, but behind the pageantry it somehow lacked the feeling which had moved her so much at her sister's wedding. The Raynhams were not churchgoers, but it would never have occurred to Juliet that there was anything incongruous about being married in a church which played no part in her life. The service over, Alex turned her attention to the hymn. She could hear no sound from Nigel, beside her, and turned to find him gazing up at the high, vaulted roof of the church. He might be admiring the architecture or working out a problem in bio-chemistry. He gave no sign of being aware of the congregation around him.

The reception was held at Fenner's, the country club to which Bruce had introduced Alex. It gave her a pang to remember that evening before her rosy dreams had shattered, although if she had been more perceptive, she would have recognised the first crack then. On the afternoon of Juliet's wedding, however, all was gaiety and glamour.

Beth, painfully shy, kept close to Alex most of the time, and when the latter was drawn off by Nigel into the garden, she sat herself on a broad window ledge, half concealed by a heavy velvet curtain, and watched the two small bridesmaids picking daisies on the lawn outside. After a little, feeling hungry, she stood up to go to the buffet for a sandwich and knocked against a figure behind her. She jumped, then blushed with confusion as she said,

"Oh, I'm so sorry. I've made you spill your drink. Let me."

Awkwardly, she mopped at the champagne trickling down the dark sleeve of a tall, burly man with a crop of black, unruly hair and a square, weather-beaten face.

"Don't worry. My fault. I didn't realise you were there."

"It couldn't be your fault. You were standing still. Let me fetch you another glass."

"No, thanks. Don't like the stuff much. Gives me a fat head."

Beth looked at the sleeve of his jacket, and crumpled the damp handkerchief in her hands as she nervously apologised again. The man's dark eyes surveyed her thoughtfully as he said,

"Don't give it another thought. I'm hungry. What about raiding those pretty dishes over there? Somehow, I'm always hungry at weddings. Not really my line of country."

"Nor mine. In fact, I'm hopeless at social functions," said Beth, amazed that she should be confiding in a stranger so easily.

"Not my strong point, either. Let's see what we can find to sustain us."

With two full plates, he suggested that they went out on to the terrace. Juliet was changing into her travelling dress and there was a hiatus to be filled. They found a seat at the far end of the terrace, and the man introduced himself.

"I'm Wainwright. Peter Wainwright. A rather remote friend of the groom's."

"And I'm Beth Raynham, Juliet's sister."

He looked surprised, and Beth concentrated her gaze on a smoked salmon sandwich, fully conscious of his unspoken comment.

"You live at Bridgefield, then. That makes us neighbours. Funny, I've never seen you around," he said.

"I don't go out much. Whereabouts in Bridgefield are you?"

"In Bathurst Lane. I'm a nurseryman."

"Bathurst Nurseries. I know it. What a wonderful show of dahlias you had last year!"

"You interested in gardening?"

"Very."

Beth's self-consciousness left her as she talked about the one real interest of her life, and time went by unnoticed.

"Why not come over and have a look round one day? You don't have to buy anything," he added with a smile.

"Thank you. I'd like to, if you're sure I shan't be a nuisance."

"Shouldn't have suggested it if I'd thought you'd be a bother. I grow a good crop of tomatoes in my greenhouse. For sale, if you ever want any."

"I'd like to buy some from you. Nothing like freshly picked tomatoes, and I don't grow any myself."

"It's a deal, then."

"Thank you, Mr Wainwright."

"Well, I suppose we'd better get back if we're to see the happy pair depart."

Beth jumped up, saying hastily,

"You must excuse me for keeping you so long. I expect I've been terribly boring, talking gardening to an expert when I'm only an ignorant amateur."

"It's never boring to talk shop. You're not very sure of yourself, are you?"

"I'm not used . . . I don't often meet anybody I can talk to."

"Nor I. Not much of a talker at all, come to that. I'm a plain man and a bit out of my element in company. I've enjoyed this little chat with you, though, Miss Raynham. And I hope I've found a new customer."

They rejoined the party a minute after Juliet and Barney had left. Beth looked at Wainwright guiltily, then gave him an odd little smile as she said,

"Well, I don't suppose I was missed."

* * *

Back at Pelham House, the residue of the wedding party settled down to enjoying themselves. They were mostly Mrs Raynham's friends, one of whom was a brilliant pianist of the light school, so that much of the evening was given over to dancing and singing.

Nigel disappeared early in the evening, before supper, and Alex, whose head was beginning to ache, watched his departure with somewhat envious eyes. The lodge would be a peaceful place. He had slipped off without a word to anybody except his mother. Lucky Nigel, who did just as he pleased.

When Bruce asked her to dance, she refused, pleading uncomfortable shoes. He followed her into the kitchen, where she went for some water, and smiled down into the sea-green eyes which studied him gravely over the glass.

"Take your shoes off, then, and dance without 'em. Here."

He swung her up on the kitchen table and took her shoes off before she could put her glass down and stop him. As she slid off the table and went to pick up the shoes, he took her in his arms.

"What's the matter, Alex? You've been giving me the cold shoulder lately."

"The less I see of you, Bruce, the better. Please let me go."

"What have I done?"

"You know all right. I suppose you think that enough time has elapsed now to make me sweet again."

"You're terribly serious, Alex. We've always been such good friends, had such fun together. What's got into you?"

"You've swopped partners, don't you remember?"

"My dear girl, you didn't take our friendship too seriously, did you? I never gave you reason to. I told you right at the start that I was out to educate you in new ways of enjoying yourself. If you read more into it than that, I'm truly sorry, but I can't feel I'm to blame. Come on, now. Kiss and be friends."

"Didn't Eve say the experimenting was to stop when you married?"

"But this is absurd. You're taking it far too seriously. Where's your sense of fun, Alex? You used to be so game."

"Yes, I was good game for you. I see that now. A green girl to be initiated. You're right. I did take you too seriously. My mistake. You're essentially a trivial person, and as such, you now bore me."

"Do I? We'll see."

He pulled her into his arms and kissed her in spite of the pummelling of her fists on his back. When he released her, she smacked his face. He stepped back, one hand fingering his marked cheek.

"You little devil."

"I'm sorry, but to feel you touch me was so revolting that I couldn't help it."

"It wasn't always so revolting."

"It is now. So keep your distance."

He laughed as she moved behind the table.

"Don't worry. I'm not interested in unwilling players. Sorry you've lost your sense of fun. I didn't educate you quite far enough, it seems. You're foolish to nurse a grievance instead of consoling yourself with what's available."

"Let's get this clear, Bruce. I don't nurse any grievance. I was a fool, and I admit it. I saw you with the silly eyes of an inexperienced girl, flattered by the attentions of a handsome young man, and not seeing that it was a game to you. But you knew I was inexperienced, and you took advantage of it just to amuse yourself, not caring about my feelings at all."

"Well, I don't see that I'm to blame if you fell for your teacher a little. It happens in all kinds of schools, you know."

"How vain and superficial you are! Don't worry. I'm quite cured."

"Then why can't we be friends again?"

"Because," said Alex slowly, "you're the first person in my life to make me feel cheap. Now, the very sight of you brings the feeling back, and to have you touch me makes me feel sick. That's final. Please go."

He shrugged his shoulders and went. Alex drew another glass of water, and drank it thirstily. Then she went upstairs to fetch a coat and some walking shoes, collected Bella and slipped out of the side door. The house seemed to be tainted with falseness and artificiality. She could hear them singing "Some Day I'll Find You" as she turned the corner of the house. The end of the wedding celebrations. You married for money, you made love for fun. A house of fun. Sickly and flabby as a marshmallow. She felt badly in need of a diet of plain, wholesome bread.

A week later, she started a fortnight's leave. She spent a few days at home, and the rest on an Exmoor farm, where she had often stayed before because the farmer and his daughter were great naturalists as well as kindly folk.

Chapter Twelve

ALEX returned to Pelham House refreshed both mentally and physically, and her welcome from Mrs Raynham was so unrestrained in its warmth that she felt again the old pull of her employer's magnetism and gaiety. Bruce and Juliet might be shallow, selfish young people, but Mrs Raynham brightened the atmosphere for everybody around her, and Alex found it impossible not to respond with affection to such warm generosity of thought and spirit.

"If you only knew how I've longed to see that bright red hair of yours about the place, dear. Not the same without you at all."

"I expect you've missed Juliet."

"Not as much as I've missed you. You're so alive. So vivacious. I *do* like live people around me. Stops me feeling mossy."

"Never have I met anybody so discouraging to moss," said Alex, laughing.

"Well, one thing became plain while you were away. Your services have become so indispensable that I'm obviously underpaying you. Not a word. I'm increasing your salary by fifty pounds a year, and at that, you're a marvellous bargain. And, with Bruce and Juliet gone, I must see that you have more time off to go out for amusement, and I shall invite more young people here for you, dear. You're much too attractive to hide your light under a bushel, you know."

With her arm through Alex's, Mrs Raynham had drawn her into the drawing-room, where tea was waiting for them.

"Beth's out, ordering plants for the garden or something. Said she mightn't be back to tea, so we won't wait. And now, tell me how you enjoyed your holiday."

Alex told her about the stags and otters and badgers, but after a few minutes of this, Mrs Raynham soon seized control of the conversation again, saying vaguely,

"How nice for you, dear! You know, I'd like to take

you abroad with me some time. The Italian Riviera. We'll plan it together some time, Alex. You mustn't stagnate here, you know. I'm a great believer in travel for young people."

She was a great believer in travel at all times, thought Alex, for Mrs Raynham never seemed to be stationary for more than an hour at one time, apart from the hours when nature forced her to sleep.

"You know, you've got us all beaten for vitality. I've never seen you tired. You have the secret of eternal youth."

"How sweet of you to say so, Alex, but I tell you when I do feel tired. When I'm bored. So I don't let myself get bored. I think most tiredness is really boredom. That's what makes housewives so often feel tired, poor dears. Such a dull life for most of them. That's why I try to cheer them up with my articles, awaken their interest in clothes and pretty things, make them think that they're part of the live world, not stuck in a backwater with a perambulator and a shopping basket for companions."

"Perhaps you only make them envious and discontented."

"Oh, no. It cheers them up, even if only for a short time. It's an escape. Anyway, anything's better than resignation. Oh, hullo, Beth dear. You said we weren't to wait, and we didn't."

"Hullo, Alex. Nice to see you back," said Beth with a smile. "I was quicker than I expected because Mr Wainwright had to go into Elton to pick up some stakes that he'd ordered, and he kindly dropped me here on his way. Have a good holiday, Alex? We've missed you."

Beth looked brighter than usual and seemed really interested in the Exmoor farm. That tea was a friendly, happy little meal, and Alex felt reassured. There had been moments at the beginning of her holiday when she had wondered whether to leave Pelham House and its reminders of Bruce's callous treatment. Now she realised that Bruce no longer mattered. She liked her job, and no employer could be more charming and appreciative than Mrs Raynham. She had allowed Bruce to upset her sense of proportion. Now, she felt quite happy to be back, with a pile of material in her field diary waiting to be written up for the *Downland Journal*.

It was not until Alex wheeled the tea trolley out to the kitchen that the spaniel realised that she had returned. Bella had been curled up asleep in her basket, and when she opened her dim eyes and saw Alex, she stared unmoving for a moment, then uttered a yelp of pleasure and half ran, half stumbled, across the floor, her body quivering with pleasure, her stump of a tail waggling the whole of her rear with its intensity.

"Dear old Bella," said Alex, putting her arms round the dog's neck. "Now don't get so excited. It's bad for you."

But Bella, panting with pleasure, seized Alex's handkerchief from her sleeve and walked round and round with it, and after this had been retrieved, she insisted on following Alex up to her room in spite of the fact that the stairs were as much as she could manage.

It was a heart-warming return, and the only person who did not fall over himself with pleasure at her reappearance was Nigel. Alex went down to the lodge after dinner that night to announce her return and present him with a letter which had been delivered to the house by mistake. She found him working, a cup of coffee beside him on the desk, which was covered with sheets of graph paper.

"Hullo, Nigel. I've brought you a letter from your love," she said blithely, for she felt very well and happy.

"Oh, hullo." He glanced at the buff envelope and threw it aside, frowning at the page of symbols in front of him. Alex though it looked like Chinese writing, but closer inspection over his shoulder revealed figures and formulæ.

"Don't loom, babe. It fidgets me."

She retreated to the arm of the sofa, on which she perched herself. He took no notice and went on plotting his graph from the details on the paper. It was a hot night, and he had bowed to the weather in so far as discarding his customary lounge suit for pale grey flannels and an immaculate white silk shirt across which flowed a lavender and grey silk tie. Piqued by his failure to remark on her return from a holiday, she swung a leg and decided to stay put until he did take notice of her presence. Nigel, however, was far more adept than she at playing a waiting game, and in the end it was Alex who broke the silence.

"You're not very polite, Nigel. You could ask me how I enjoyed my holiday."

"How did you?"

"Very much, thanks."

"A stock question, a stock reply. Rather pointless, I always think."

After a few minutes, she tried again.

"No wonder you always look so sallow, spending so much time indoors working. What a way of spending a lovely summer night!"

"What would you suggest? A nice walk in the country, looking for toads with you and Bella?"

"You could do worse," she said, smiling.

"Run away, babe. I'm busy."

She moved across the room to a small picture hanging over the fireplace. She had not seen it there before and she studied it intently. Nigel was, she knew, a great lover of the visual arts, and his taste embraced paintings, sculpture and architecture. This little oil painting was of a landscape at dusk: a clearing in some woods, the trees bare against the wintry sky, a suggestion of frost on the rutted ground, and a crescent moon like a gondola just glimmering above the tree in the fading light. She found it oddly entrancing, and she said so.

"He's captured the mood exactly. That last brooding light on a winter's day." She peered at the signature in the corner, but did not recognise the name. "Is he a contemporary painter, Nigel?"

"Yes. Friend of mine. Just had his first show in London. I think he's exceptionally good."

"So do I. He reminds me of Constable in the way he feels the country. It's clear that he loves it deeply."

"I'll tell him," said Nigel, grinning. "He'll certainly be flattered."

"Well, I dare say it sounded silly, but I'm not knowledgeable about art. That's how it strikes me." She stood back from the picture, her head on one side, and added reflectively, "I love that moment, just before night falls. Sometimes it's so lovely that you could cry."

"Why?"

"Oh, I don't know. Because we're so ugly and understand so little, perhaps."

"You can always cheer yourself up by thinking of Michael Angelo and Constable and Shakespeare and Beethoven. A few emerge from the shabby ruck."

She turned and looked at him with a grave smile.

"You *do* understand, don't you?"

"I have faint glimmerings, babe," he said, grinning.

"Well, I wish I could afford to buy a picture like that."

"You know, you are a most disturbing object to have about the place. You will involve me in some deep philosophical discussion at the most inopportune times; when I'm driving or bogged down in some tricky bit of analysis. Tonight is not my night for visitors."

"That is moderately clear."

He leaned back in his chair, surveying her with his fingertips pressed together, like a headmaster tackling a difficult pupil.

"Then why haven't you taken the hint?"

"It wasn't subtle enough. And, anyway, I thought politeness called for some acknowledgment of my return. Everybody else has given me such a warm welcome."

"I am not everybody else. This is my haven from everybody else, and you invade it as though you belong here."

He was speaking in the half mocking, half amused way he so often used with her, but it was not without its tinge of friendly understanding.

"How very impertinent of me!" she said, her eyes dancing.

"It is. Be off with you."

She lingered by the door, a little forlornly, making a vivid panel of colour against the dove-grey paintwork. Her hair was burnished by the amber wall lights above, which deepened the primrose colour of the cotton frock she wore, and turned the blue cardigan which she had knotted carelessly round her neck by the sleeves into the same blue-green colour as her eyes. An arresting young creature. For a moment he allowed his mind to wander to Bruce. No wonder . . . He recalled his thoughts to sterner subjects.

"Thanks for bringing the letter."

"You don't feel like a breath of fresh air with Bella and me, then?"

"No, woman. Get you behind me."

"Another time, friend of mine," retorted Alex, flashing him a smile.

"Hi, just a minute." Alex's head popped back round the door. "I'm meeting Guy at the house next Saturday afternoon, and going back to spend the evening with them. Jane asked me to bring you along if you were free, and willing. What about it?"

"Love to. Thanks."

"Thank Jane, not me."

"Shall I spoil your day?"

"I'll grin and bear it. Tell Ben I'd like another cup of coffee as you go out, will you?"

* * *

On the following Friday afternoon, Alex drove Beth over to the Bathurst Nurseries to fetch a bale of peat and some tomatoes. As always, Beth apologised profusely for troubling her.

"Are you sure you can spare the time?"

"Absolutely. Your mother left me very little work to do this morning, and my own article has just gone off to Mr Barling. Besides, I'm curious to see these nurseries that you find so fascinating," said Alex, teasing her a little, and then regretting it as Beth flushed and said,

"I like to deal with Mr Wainwright. He's so helpful, and perhaps my little bit of custom helps. I hope he won't think I'm taking too much advantage of his kindness."

"Why should he?"

Beth was silent, and Alex went to fetch the car. When she

brought it round to the house, she found Beth waiting with a pile of newspapers to put on the back seat and a curious set expression on her face.

"Mother won't thank us if we make the back of the car peaty," she said as she arranged the papers. Her voice was a little muffled as she added, "Would you mind terribly if I asked you to fetch the tomatoes and peat without me? I've a good deal of ironing to do this afternoon."

Alex waited until Beth emerged from the back of the car, then said flatly,

"I should mind, and I'm counting on you to show me round the nurseries and introduce me to Mr Wainwright. I liked the look of him at the wedding, though I never had a chance to talk to him. Hop in."

"I don't think I will, Alex."

"Why not? Don't tell me about the ironing again."

"Well, I don't want him to think I'm always hanging round. Perhaps I've been making myself a bit conspicuous."

"My dear girl, what are nurseries for if not to welcome interested buyers? You really are too morbidly self-conscious for words."

"You don't understand, Alex. After that dreadful affair with Harry, I couldn't bear anybody to think . . . I'm so afraid of embarrassing Mr Wainwright by pushing myself forward. There's nothing foolish about it, of course. I'm interested in gardening and he really does seem helpful, but perhaps I'm just being a nuisance. I've only small orders to give and I don't suppose they're much help."

"They all add up. Don't be a chump, Beth. You really do make things hard for yourself. If Mr Wainwright has been kind enough to help you with advice, it's because he likes giving advice. We all do, come to that. So stop thinking about yourself and come and show me the Bathurst Nurseries."

Beth allowed herself to be persuaded, but she was stiff and ill at ease when Peter Wainwright walked round with them, a fact which Alex tried to hide by chattering blithely. She liked this sensible, burly man, and thought he was the last type to allow himself to be imposed upon, which opinion she made clear to Beth on the way home.

"He's a man of mature years, and he won't thank you for behaving like a shy adolescent."

"Are they shy these days?"

"Well, you're in no danger of being labelled a brassy hussy, but the reverse can be just as tiresome, I guess. Peter Wainwright is a down-to-earth type who obviously likes people to meet him on his own level."

"You don't know how hard it is when you've no self-confidence. I can't forget how Juliet laughed that night. I don't expect you remember. I shan't ever forget. To look such a fool. To be so ridiculous."

Alex, wishing passionately to rid Beth of this crippling inferiority complex, found it hard to forgive her family for their thoughtless treatment over the years. Her own recent humiliation at Bruce's hands made her sympathise with Beth's, but she knew that she had emerged practically unscathed compared with Beth.

"We all make fools of ourselves sometimes," she said gently. "I did, over Bruce. I haven't wanted to talk about it, but I'll admit it now to you if it makes you feel less of an isolated case."

"I wondered. You were together so much. But it's different for you. You're lively and attractive and people like you. There will be other men for you."

"Never," said Alex firmly. "I've finished with them. It's a career for me."

"I wonder. Anyway, I shall have no choice. I'm nearly thirty, I'm plain and dull and awkward. I don't mind. I've accepted it now, that no man will ever want to marry me. It's just that I'm so afraid of being thought . . . Well, what the family thought I was over Harry. I suppose they were right, too. I believed that I loved him, but it was only wishful thinking. I wanted to have a home, a life of my own, away from a family so gifted and attractive that they always serve as a bitter contrast."

It was difficult to see how the damage done over the years

could ever be wiped out, but Alex found herself wondering
how Mrs Raynham could not have seen the damage, and she
thanked providence, not for the first time since her arrival at
Pelham House, for having bestowed on her a sounder family
background. Beth was in a prison which she was afraid to
escape from, and Alex decided, with the same ardour with
which she would have gone to the rescue of a trapped animal,
that something would have to be done about it.

Chapter Thirteen

NIGEL's house was up to roof level, and Alex was able to
appreciate the front elevation, with its high gable and silver-
grey half timbering. A terrace was being planned by Nigel and
a landscape gardener to run along the back of the house, and
Alex drifted away while they discussed the niceties of various
types of stone, and strolled to the wild end of the garden to
see if the family of hedgehogs was about. The heat wave was
unbroken, and the leaves on trees and bushes were motionless.
The sky was a glassy blue, as though clouds were unknown to
it. Beneath the trees, the shade embraced her, and she would
have liked to lie down in the long, cool grass and let the
summer afternoon glide over her. She was a little put out with
Nigel, who had hustled her off immediately after lunch to
meet Guy and the landscape gardener earlier than originally
planned. She had learned during the rather breathless drive
that this was because Guy had arranged a foursome at golf to
include Nigel that afternoon, and Alex was to be deposited
with Jane on their way to the golf course. They would
be back to a late supper that night. Alex could not see why
she should feel a little disgruntled with these plans, but she
did.

When Nigel shouted her name, she walked back in a
leisurely manner which caused him to say,

"Come on, babe. We haven't all day."

"I have. You should have posted me on, Nigel, and then you could have gone straight to your golf."

He gave her a quick glance, but Guy joined them before he could reply, and in a few moments they went off, Guy leading the way in his car. Any feeling that she had been hauled in as a sop for Jane while the two men went off to golf, however, was dissipated in the sincere warmth of Jane's friendliness, and the two girls spent a happy afternoon together walking over the heath close to the Carstairs' home with Jane's two golden retrievers. They sat in the garden in the evening, a jug of iced home-made lemonade beside them, until the sun went down in a fiery glow and they went indoors to prepare a cold supper.

The men returned in high fettle, having beaten their opponents, and the supper party was a jolly one. With tongues enlivened by wine, Guy and Jane needled Nigel about his coming solitary rule of the new house.

"Why all those rooms for one man and his aide? I'd never dare call Ben a servant. I believe you're going to lord it over a harem, Nigel," said Jane, her eyes sparkling.

"Could be," said Nigel imperturbably.

"What are you going to call it?" asked Guy. "The Citadel?"

"Haven't decided yet."

"Now, honestly, Nigel, wouldn't you like to come home to a nice cosy little woman waiting there every night, with your glass of sherry ready?"

"Ben is wonderfully efficient, and he doesn't talk."

"Is it really a matter of choice, your bachelor state, or is it that the right woman hasn't turned up?" asked Jane.

"Firm choice. I am not a domestic type, and I should loathe having my life disturbed by a cosy little woman. After all," he added slyly, "I don't have to marry to get a housekeeper."

"Shame on you. Doesn't sentiment enter into your calculations at all?"

"Where would I be if it did? At the mercy of the hunting Eve. You need to be well armoured to escape their cunning strategy, and it's no good opening wide eyes at me, Jane. You're my favourite woman, but I wouldn't let you wheedle me an inch from my stronghold."

"You really are a hardened case."

"Like the cat, I prefer to walk alone. I know my self-sufficiency must be very irritating."

"It could be a challenge," said Jane thoughtfully.

"Can you be so sure that you're immune from the fever?" asked Alex. "You may think you're a sensible, level-headed person, and suddenly you find yourself enmeshed just like all the silly infatuated people you've scorned before."

"Whose side are you on, for heaven's sake?" asked Jane, smiling, but Alex knew that Nigel understood.

"There's only one thing to do, babe, when you feel yourself slipping. Run for it. It doesn't do to underestimate the low cunning of nature to achieve her ends."

"I think you're right," said Alex gravely, and they all laughed at her solemnity.

How could you recognise the gold from the dross, she wondered, as the others went on talking. What could be built on, and what was shifting sand? She had sincerely thought that she loved Bruce, and realised now that his loss had meant little more than hurt pride. She seldom gave him a thought now, and yet, at the time, he had seemed so all-absorbing. She supposed it would be called an infatuation. The sort of thing indulged in by silly girls, not sensible young women like Alex Madison. It was all very undermining. Nigel was right. Best run away from such dangerous indulgences.

Driving back to Pelham House with him, Alex asked,

"Have you ever had to run away, Nigel?"

He thought a moment, for Alex had the habit of suddenly reverting to a conversation which had ceased hours ago, then said,

"Yes. Once."

"Long ago?"

"Four or five years."

"Isn't it terribly difficult to know the moment at which to run? I mean, it's an insidious sort of thing, isn't it?"

"Very. In this case, we'd made a contract from the start. I ran when she began to break the terms."

"Hearts won't work to contract, unfortunately."

"You're in an unusually serious mood today. No butterflies or rare birds to report?"

"We saw a young fox on the heath this afternoon. Have you ever seen one running? They move so beautifully."

When she had told him about the fox, she relapsed into silence. It was a warm, breathless night. The heat-wave would be bound to end in a storm, she thought, as her eyes watched the headlights skimming over the hedgerows of the narrow lane. Thinking of Nigel's admission, she cast a quick glance at his hawk-like profile. It might have been carved of stone. His hands on the wheel were slender, with long fingers, but gave an impression of strength and competence in spite of their elegance. What an odd mixture he was, she thought. A scientist with artistic tastes, a ruthless egoist, but not callous about other people's feelings, as she had once thought. She wondered who had caused him to run. He could be very attractive to women, she decided. His very independence of them would prove a bait. She wondered just what the terms of that contract had been. Whatever else one experienced with Nigel, it would never be boredom, she decided as the car turned into the drive of Pelham House.

"Why didn't you choose to go home this week-end?" he asked.

"Too much work to do. Your mother has been in London most of this week, and she hasn't had a chance to deal with her articles or any correspondence. I said I'd work tomorrow, as I was booked with the Carstairs this afternoon."

"Working on a Sunday. Dear me. Against all union rules."

"Don't you ever work on Sunday?"

"Invariably. I hope you enjoyed your day."

"Very much. Jane's so nice."

"Yes, she is. A real poppet. All in darkness. Have you got your key?"

"Yes, thanks. Good night, Nigel."

She slid out of the car and he drove it off to the garage behind the lodge. As she walked up the drive, looking at the black velvet sky pricked with stars, she found herself envying again Nigel's control of his life. He drove it as he drove his car, swiftly, easily, and with superb confidence. She was like an inept cyclist, dashing into prickly hedges, or wobbling all over the road.

* * *

A few days later, Beth was thrown into a state of excitement by an invitation from Wainwright to go to a horticultural show in London at which he was exhibiting.

"He's asked me to go up early and help him arrange the stand," said Beth to Alex.

"What fun! You'll be rather good at it, judging by your skill at arranging a supper table for festive occasions."

"The only thing is, I'll have to tell Mother. I'll be away all day, and there's lunch to think of. I could leave something cold all ready for you. You don't know if Mother's going to be in London tomorrow, do you?"

"I'm not sure."

"I'd rather she didn't know about this, but I suppose that's foolish. My family have a way of passing little remarks that somehow take the shine off things for me."

"I'm sure your mother will be pleased to think of you having a day out. Heaven knows you get little enough change."

And, indeed, Mrs Raynham's reaction was kind enough when Beth told her, faltering a little and pushing nervously at her glasses.

"How very nice for you, darling! Tomorrow. Let me see. I shall be having lunch with David Barling. We've a lot to talk about in connection with the next number of the journal. I think you'll have to cut your column, Alex, because I want a special summer holiday supplement."

"I'll leave something cold for you, Alex, then," said Beth.

"Don't worry about me. I can cook myself an omelette."

"That's right. You go off and enjoy yourself, Beth, dear. It will be a nice change for you."

To Beth's relief, her mother said no more, but before she started dictating some letters to Alex, Mrs Raynham asked her about Peter Wainwright.

"What sort of a person is he, Alex? You went over there the other day, I believe."

"Yes. I liked him. A very responsible, honest sort of person."

"How old?"

"Perhaps forty. Difficult to say with that stolid type. Didn't you see him at the wedding?"

"No. I didn't get round to him. I hope Beth's not going to make a fool of herself again, poor dear. She does get so worked up if a man says a word to her."

Alex looked down at her notebook, hesitating to reveal more. It was foreign to her nature not to be frank, but something held her back, and she contented herself with drawing squiggles at the side of her notebook. Mrs Raynham, however, was not to be put off.

"Do you think she's losing her head again, Alex?"

"No. And Mr Wainwright is far too mature a person to make that kind of foolishness admissible. You need have no anxiety on that score, I'm sure."

"Good. Now, a letter to David first. I want him to have it before I arrive tomorrow morning, to give him time to digest my suggestions. He's such an old stick-in-the-mud that he needs lots of warning when new ideas are broached. They may have taken root a little by the time I arrive and stop him saying, as he usually does, 'Now, my dear lady, this is Bridgefield, not London.' I could scream when he says that. He's so parochial, but his readers aren't necessarily so limited, as I keep on telling him."

* * *

Beth returned from her day in London, tired and happy, with the news that Peter had won a medal for his display of sweet peas. Her pride and pleasure in this suggested that, whether she admitted it or not, Beth had grown very fond of Wainwright.

"Now I'm for bed," she said. "My legs ache as though I'd

walked thirty miles. It was so interesting seeing all those garden-lovers there, and chatting to those who came to our stand. Then afterwards, we went and had a delightful dinner in a quiet little Italian restaurant Peter knew. I haven't enjoyed myself so much for ages. In fact, it's been the happiest day I can ever remember."

Only to Alex did Beth open up in this way, and when she heard her parents arriving back from a bridge party, she slipped off hurriedly, saying to Alex,

"Tell Mother I've gone to bed, and just say I had an interesting day, if she asks."

Mrs Raynham did ask, and Alex gave her the non-committal message, feeling uneasy because it seemed necessary to protect Beth. It was rare indeed for Mr Raynham to accompany his wife on a social occasion, for they led separate lives to a great extent. Sometimes it seemed as though he was a resident in a hotel, so remote did he keep from his family and their concerns. Only in crises was he called upon to support his wife, which he did with great efficiency in order to be able to return to his sphere of business as quickly as possible. Alex could only conclude that an exception had been made this evening because their host was a stockbroker who might be a useful man to know.

Mrs Raynham looked very lovely in a black silk dress which emphasised her fair skin, and moulded her slender figure. She wore pearl ear-rings and four rows of pearls round her neck. Her fair hair shone in the light from the chandelier, and Alex marvelled again at the youthful looks Beth's mother had preserved. Juliet would probably be like her at that age. Fair, lovely and untouched. And would she have children who needed defences against her?

"I do hope we don't have a storm," said Mrs Raynham, "but I believe I heard rumblings in the distance just now. Alex, my dear, you look tired and ought to be in bed. It's half-past eleven."

Before getting into bed, Alex sat on the window-seat for a little, watching the play of lightning in the distance. The atmosphere was too close and oppressive to sleep, and if the storm reached them, she would have to fetch Bella from the kitchen, for the old spaniel was terrified of storms. As she watched, she saw headlights turn into the drive, and Nigel's black Jaguar drew up just past the lodge. To her surprise, she saw a girl emerge from it and stand waiting while the car was driven into the garage. Then Nigel's tall figure rejoined her, and, putting an arm round her shoulder, he hurried her into the lodge. That diminutive figure had been Jane's, Alex felt sure. She watched the lights flash on in the lodge. Soon she saw the upstairs lights go on, too. Then there was darkness.

She did not know how long she sat there, remembering that Ben was on holiday this week and Guy away on a job in the west country. When the storm broke over Bridgefield, she went downstairs and collected the whimpering Bella, who licked her hand with trembling eagerness and plodded up the stairs at her heels so closely that she nearly tripped Alex up.

Rain was streaming down now, bringing with it a freshening of the air which made Alex reluctant to close the window, although the rain was splashing through on to the window seat. The lodge was still in darkness. Her head was aching and she suddenly felt tired to death. Leaving the small ventilator open, she closed the curtains and switched on the bedside lamp to off-set the lightning which upset Bella so much, soothed the spaniel as well as she could, and tumbled into bed, whereat Bella immediately startled scrabbling at the sheet. In the end, she was persuaded to lie down on the rug beside the bed, and Alex lay back, her only covering a sheet, trying to stop pictures forming in her mind of the couple in the lodge. The thunder became a distant intermittent rumble, but the rain rustled down as though it never meant to stop.

Chapter Fourteen

IN the morning, Alex was heavy-eyed and pale, but was able to explain it by the storm. She had seen Nigel's car go off early that morning. Toying with her breakfast, she felt sick with misery. Nothing that had happened to her in this house so far had stabbed her as deeply as this. So devastating was the damage to her heart and mind that she could not contemplate it or attempt to sum it up. She merely endured a kind of death inside her as an animal will endure sickness in stoical acceptance.

In spite of trying to pin her mind on her work, the day dragged interminably, and Mrs Raynham stopped her from doing any more after tea, advising her to take some aspirins and lie down until dinner. Inaction, however, was intolerable, and she collected Bella and took her across the common. She was unlucky enough to return just after Nigel arrived home, and could not avoid meeting him face to face as he came out of the garage.

"Good lord!" he exclaimed. "You look terrible. What's the matter?"

"The storm last night kept me awake. I had to fetch Bella up with me. She gets in a frightful flap in storms."

"Poor babe. You look as though you've been dehydrated, like a prune."

She avoided his eyes, and said hurriedly,

"I must fly or I'll be late for dinner."

She half ran up the drive with Bella panting behind her, and was able to avoid contact with Nigel again until the following week, when she felt a little better armoured. This time, it was through Ben that she was brought face to face with him, for she had determined to avoid him at all costs. On that Monday afternoon she was alone in the house, typing in her office, when Ben appeared at the open window.

"Hullo, Ben. Did you have a good holiday?"

"Fine, Miss Madison, thanks. Nothing like the Welsh

mountains, you know. Hope I'm not disturbing your work, but I find I've got to slip down to the village, and I wondered whether you'd do me a favour."

"Of course."

"We're expecting delivery of a Florentine mirror from some London sale rooms. Should have arrived this morning, but it didn't, and I'll wager it'll come while I'm in the village. If it does, could you see it in for me? I'll leave a note on the front door of the lodge, telling them to call here for instructions."

"Right you are. Is it to go anywhere special?"

"In the front bedroom. That's where we're packing the bits and pieces his nibs is collecting for his new house. At least, we started off parking them in my room, but I'm a bit cluttered up now, and if anything else goes in there, I'll never get to my bed. The side door will be unlocked. Leave it all to the men. It'll be heavy. Just see that they stow it in safely. Of course, they may not come before I'm back, but I thought I'd better make provision in case they do."

"All right, Ben. I'll see to it."

"Much obliged, Miss Madison."

The men arrived ten minutes after Ben had gone, and Alex supervised the delivery. It was a large package and required two men to carry it. She conducted them to the bedroom and they propped it against the wall behind a small chest of drawers. While they were doing this, they dislodged a narrow strip of pink silk, and Alex picked it up and laid it on the bed. It looked as though it was the belt off a nightdress. When she had signed for the mirror and seen the men off, she returned to the room and picked up the belt. Ben would undoubtedly check that the mirror had been safely stowed away, and she hesitated to leave the belt there. It would be best, perhaps, to take it and lose it. As she stood there, fingering the silk, she heard a car and saw the Jaguar draw up outside. What on earth could have brought Nigel home at this hour of the afternoon? In a sudden panic, she flew down the stairs and dived into the dining-room just as Nigel came into the hall. She hid behind the door as he went upstairs, and was about to creep out when she thought she heard him coming down again. Without stopping to think that it would be simpler to explain her presence and make a quick return to her work, she decided to go out of the window, for the idea of facing him was more than she could stomach. She was halfway through the window when her ankle was seized and Nigel's amazed voice said,

"What on earth goes on?"

He shifted his grip to her waist and swung her back into the room, where she looked at him helplessly, the pink silk belt still clenched in one hand.

"Won't you enlighten me?" he asked coolly.

"Ben asked me to see your mirror in if it arrived while he was in the village. It did. They've put it in your bedroom."

"And why the unorthodox exit?"

She was silent while he studied her thoughtfully, then he went on:

"It's not like you to be at a loss for words. It needs no great powers of deduction to arrive at the fact that you were trying to avoid me. Correct?"

"Yes."

"And now I come to think of it, you've been avoiding me for the past week. What's the matter, Alex?"

"Nothing I want to talk about."

"That won't do, you know."

"Why are you home so early?"

"Had a raging toothache all the morning. Couldn't stick it any longer and I've just had it out at the dentist's. It was a bit of a do. Took him quarter of an hour. A wisdom tooth. So I thought I'd call it a day."

"I'm sorry. Ben will be back soon, I expect."

"I can exist without him. I was just going upstairs to rinse out my mouth when I heard something in here. Now it's your turn."

"Go and see to your mouth, Nigel. I must get back to my typewriter."

"You're not going, my child, until you tell me what's bitten you," he said, sitting down on the arm of a chair and retaining her hand.

She knew from his face that she was caught, and although she searched her mind for some garbled story to tell him, she knew that between them there could be nothing but the truth. She made one more appeal.

"Please let me go, Nigel. I'll explain another time."

"Give me whatever it is you're fidgeting with."

She handed him the belt in silence.

"Well, well. How come? Does it keep up something of vital importance?"

"I found it in your bedroom. The men pushed it out from behind the chest of drawers."

"Well, I wonder how it got there." He eyed it, stretching it out to its full length. "Of course. Jane's. I'd say it was the belt of a nightie, wouldn't you?"

"Yes." He had spoken as though nightdress belts were as common as daisies in his room.

"She must have left it last week. Funny she didn't telephone about it. I'll be seeing Guy at the site tomorrow evening. I'll hand it over then."

Alex's eyes by now were nearly popping out of her head, and he could not fail to notice her amazement. He leaned against the back of the chair as he stowed the belt in his pocket, and said quietly with a look in his narrowed eyes which she didn't much like,

"What's in your mind, Alex?"

He had released her and she turned aside and looked out of the window as though seeking inspiration there. At last she said haltingly,

"Won't Guy think it odd that you should have it?"

"Not if his wife left it in my bedroom when they stayed here last Tuesday night."

"Did they borrow your car, too?"

"They did. I could explain why, but at this moment I don't feel inclined to. Why have you been avoiding me all the week, and why did you put on this lunatic act this afternoon? My patience is running out, Alex. A plain answer, please."

She looked at him warily, her heart lightened so that it felt like a balloon soaring heavenwards after being tethered in a dungeon of Stygian gloom. She decided that she could wriggle out of this with a little skill, and gave him a wide smile which did not appear to charm him as she had hoped.

"Oh, just a little misunderstanding, Nigel. And I've been in an odd mood since that storm. I think it unnerved me. Forget it."

"Not on your life. I dare you to have the courage of your opinions."

"Not accepted. We all make mistakes."

"You saw them arrive in my car, I suppose."

"Yes."

"And you saw Jane?"

"Yes."

"And Guy?"

"Yes, I saw them both."

"But you didn't think it was Guy."

"Oh, Nigel, must you be like a ferret?"

"I've told you before, I like getting at the truth. I suppose Guy and I are much the same build, and from a distance, coming from my car. . . . Was that it?"

"Yes, if you must know."

"Where were *you*?"

"I was sitting by my bedroom window watching the storm over the hills. It was too hot to sleep and I wanted to keep an eye on Bella if the storm came our way."

"And the car stayed there all night. Did you keep watch to see when it went?" he asked sardonically.

"I saw it go in the morning," she said, flushing.

"What a busy night you must have had! I must confess I don't see why you were creeping out just now with the incriminating evidence, nor why you were unwilling to face me and denounce me with your usual vigour."

His face was white and she realised that, for the first time since she had known him, he was really angry. One cheek was badly swollen. That, obviously, was not helping to sweeten his attitude.

"I thought it better that Ben shouldn't find it."

"How considerate of you! I seem to have taught you your

lesson too well, Alex. From wide-eyed trust, you now seem to have dived to the other extreme."

"What else could I believe on that evidence? Was it likely that your friends would be sleeping at the lodge that night instead of you? I knew that Ben was away, and that Guy, according to what he told us when we were over there, was on a job in the west country."

"That was postponed."

"Well, what would you have believed if you'd seen what I saw? The facts were there. Or seemed to be."

"You didn't think of querying them with me. You believed that I was having an affair with my friend's wife as soon as his back was turned. If you didn't credit me with any better principles, you might have credited Jane with some. It's inconceivable, knowing them both, as you do. And you didn't even question me about it. Thanks, Alex, for the compliment."

"You're terribly angry about it, aren't you? Well, I suppose you've a right to be. I'm sorry."

"That's a bit inadequate, isn't it? Perhaps I'd better tell you what did happen in case you still harbour doubts."

"It doesn't matter."

"Isn't that rash of you? After all, I might be bluffing."

"I know you wouldn't lie about it. Please don't be so cruel, Nigel. I've said I'm sorry. I can't undo it."

"I'd better tell all, or the wrong version may get around."

She swung round on him then, her eyes flashing.

"How dare you say that! You know I would never have breathed a word to anybody."

"You see, you don't like the slightest aspersion cast on your character, but you expect me to smile it off when you throw buckets of mud at Jane and me. As it happened, I was at a dinner in London that evening and stayed the night at the hotel where the dinner was held. For reasons which I won't bother to explain, it was convenient for Guy and Jane to borrow my car and bedroom in my absence. Perhaps you would like me to give you the name of the hotel where I stayed, so that you can check my story."

"No, of course not," said Alex wretchedly, wishing she

could think of something to take that icy expression from his face.

"Or you can ask Jane," he said sardonically.

"Don't be so deadly about it, please. I was a fool. I know I'm always jumping to wrong conclusions, and I'm terribly sorry about this one. But I do think I had a little excuse."

"But none for not giving me the benefit of a doubt and asking me about it."

"I couldn't talk about it," she said simply, trying to explain the mood of complete desolation which had swept over her. "I'd come to this house, seeing it as a Utopia, a land of smiles, as my brother put it. I've found out, bit by bit, that the smiles were unreliable, as you warned me. But I've always felt that I stood on firm ground as I looked around. After that night . . ." she faltered, then went on without looking at him, "after that night, I felt as though there was no ground under my feet any more. I'd fallen down a great chasm. That's why I couldn't ask any questions or reason about it at all. I didn't sit in judgment on you or Jane. Not consciously, anyway. I just felt hopelessly lost. It's hard to explain to you, because you're so rational in your attitude to everything, and I'm . . . well, my feelings easily swamp my reason. But that's how it was."

As she lifted her eyes to his, she realised with relief that his cold anger had receded while she spoke. Instead, he wore a rather odd expression as he looked at her. Then he stood up and put a hand on her shoulder.

"All right. Let's forget it. I've a filthy headache and I feel as thought I've been socked in the jaw by a champion heavyweight. I'm going to have a clean up."

"Can I make you some tea?"

"Here's Ben. He'll do it, thanks. Lord, what a day!" he added, feeling his jaw gingerly.

And then Ben came in, concerned at finding Nigel there looking so much the worse for wear, and Alex went back to her work, feeling badly in need of a cup of tea herself.

Chapter Fifteen

SEPTEMBER came in with some glorious days of sunshine after early morning mist, and Alex welcomed the added freshness of the air. A vague feeling of foreboding had hovered over her recently, and she found herself counting the days to Nigel's departure like a miser counting his coins. Since her blunder, she had sensed a change in him, although he had not referred to it again. She did not see much of him, and when they met, he seemed guarded, as he had never been before. He had not forgiven her, she felt.

Beneath Mrs Raynham's gaiety, too, Alex felt a certain wary alertness towards Beth, who seemed to alternate between moods of happiness and gloom. In fact, things were in a state of uneasy flux, and Alex found it very irksome.

Beth had achieved marvels in the garden of Pelham House that summer, and it was now full of colour from dahlias, roses, petunias and marigolds, so that Alex, thinking to cheer her up as she helped her cut off the dead heads from the dahlias one evening, said,

"You should ask Peter to come and see your results, Beth. I'm sure they'd impress him."

"I don't suppose I shall be seeing him again," said Beth gruffly, as she stooped to pick up a fallen flower head.

"Why ever not? You're such good friends."

"He's moving. He's never had enough ground there. Now he's bought ten acres in Kent."

"When does he go?"

"I don't know exactly, but soon, I think. He was telling me about it when some people arrived to see over the Nurseries, and he had to go."

Before Alex could commiserate with her, Beth walked quickly away towards the toolshed. At dinner, Mrs Raynham brought up the subject.

"I hear Bathurst Nurseries are up for sale, Beth. Is that right?"

"Yes."

"Dear me. Don't tell me that your friend has gone broke."

"No. He's done rather well, I believe. He's moving to a bigger place in Kent."

"Whereabouts?"

"I don't know, Mother. After all, it's none of my business."

"Don't be so grumpy, darling. I thought that, as you were a pretty regular visitor, he might have told you."

"Well, he hasn't, and I don't intend to ask. People are always poking their noses into other people's business in Bridgefield. I never knew such a place."

"It's inevitable in small places."

"Would you like coffee in here or in the drawing-room?" asked Beth, her face grim and shuttered.

"In the drawing-room, darling, I think."

Mrs Raynham sighed as Beth went out of the room to fetch the coffee.

"What a prickly creature she is, to be sure. Poor Beth. I'm afraid she may have been indulging in day-dreams again."

Why always "Poor Beth", thought Alex angrily. Why couldn't she accord her daughter some dignity?

"What do you think, Alex?" asked Mrs Raynham delicately.

"About what?" asked Alex, who could be as obtuse as a block of wood if she chose.

"About Beth and Wainwright. Did she entertain any ideas in that quarter, do you think?"

"Not that I've heard of."

Nothing more was said about the matter that evening. Beth went round with a stony, impassive face for the rest of the week, avoiding her mother and Alex as much as possible. Alex, aching to help, but fearing to make matters worse, watched her with sympathetic eyes.

On the following Monday morning, a telephone call came from Peter Wainwright. Alex was in the study, taking dictation, when Mrs Raynham answered it.

"Oh, yes. Mr Wainwright, did you say? . . . Yes, I believe I have, now you come to mention it. . . . I'm afraid she's not here at the moment. Can I take a message for her? . . . Yes,

I'll tell her as soon as she comes in. . . . No, I'm sure she hasn't. . . . Goodbye."

Beth's appointment with the optician had taken her to the village that morning. Her mother might have sounded a little more expansive, Alex thought. She had behaved as though Wainwright's name was unknown in the house.

"I shan't answer this naughty letter of David's," said Mrs Raynham mischievously, "I shall just let him stew. No, just a minute. I'll send him an extra sweet covering letter with my article, as though I'd never received his. And we'll ask kindly after his lumbago."

Alex smiled and shook her head as she began to take the letter down. Her employer's running battle with her editor was conducted with all the charm in the world, but she never gave an inch.

At lunch, Mrs Raynham told Beth that Mr Wainwright had telephoned to say goodbye.

"He was sorry to miss you, darling, but he hadn't had a chance to telephone before, he's been so busy packing up."

"I didn't expect him to," said Beth briefly. "Is he leaving today, then?"

"I gathered so. You'll have to see what the new people are like, Beth. I hope their tomatoes will be as good. We've never had such fine ones as Wainwright's."

"He's good at his job. I didn't change my frames, after all, Mother. I thought the present ones were all right."

"Oh, Beth, why didn't you have a more modern style? They can be so attractive these days. Those old horn-rimmed frames of yours are so heavy for you."

"I'm used to them."

"Well, just have your spare pair framed attractively, then. You'll be taking those you're wearing now to have new lenses fitted when you get the other pair back, won't you?"

"Yes."

"Then I shall come with you and choose a really becoming frame for you. A light colour and not that old-fashioned oval shape."

"It means having different shaped lenses."

"Well, we'll have them, then," said her mother impatiently.

"It's no good, Mother. You can't glamorise me with a pair of fancy spectacles," said Beth with a wry little smile.

"How stubborn you are, Beth, and quite wrong about yourself, you know. I've learned by now that it's no use lecturing you, though. Now, it's a glorious day and I insist on you two girls going out into the country this afternoon. I've no urgent work for Alex, and you look washed out, Beth. An afternoon in the sun will do you both a world of good. Take your tea with you and make a picnic of it."

"What about it, Beth? It is a lovely day," said Alex, thinking that it might help Beth to loose that tense look.

"You're not even to ask her, Alex, or she'll find a list of chores as long as my arm to keep her home. Why not take the car to the foot of Furze Hill, and walk up to the top for your picnic? It's lovely up there. I'd come, too, but it's nose to the grindstone for me this afternoon. Three articles to get down on paper."

Gaily, she arranged it all for them, and at half-past two they were ready. Mrs Raynham stood at the door waving them off, but Alex had driven no farther than the village when Beth, who had been strangely silent ever since lunch, said suddenly,

"It's no good, Alex. I'm sorry, but would you mind dropping me off at the common? I want to be alone."

Her voice trembled on the last words and she was wringing her hands together in a kind of frenzied desperation. Alex said nothing, but drew up as the village fell behind them.

"It's Peter, isn't it?"

"No," said Beth, fiercely. "No. It's me. I'm getting neurotic, I guess."

"You don't have to pretend with me, Beth. I wouldn't tell anybody. I think you love Peter Wainwright. What is there to be ashamed of in that?"

"No. It's just that I can't face life going on in the same old way, day after day, without even the Nurseries to go to. He was so kind, and, somehow, interested. Nobody has ever really been interested in me. It was so . . . heartening. And now, it's all empty again. I don't think I can bear it, and yet I know I shall. Just now, though, I want to walk on my own until I can accept it."

"Why didn't you go to the Nurseries last week, as it was his last one as owner?"

"And embarrass him? I'd rather die. I couldn't hide my unhappiness from him. If I've nothing else left, I have my pride. I'll never embarrass another man again. He's been kind to me, but I was just a casual friend, that's all. Nothing much when you've plenty of friends and a full life. But to me, that little meant . . . everything."

"He may have expected you to go and say goodbye."

"Well, he did it over the 'phone, so that's good enough. Forgive me for going off, Alex, but I must be alone."

"All right. What about the tea?"

"You have it."

"Beth, you're not going to do anything silly, are you?"

Beth smiled a sad little smile that went to Alex's heart.

"I'm not the dramatic sort, Alex. No, I shall be back on duty at Pelham House tonight, as usual."

Alex watched her plod away over the common, head down, her cotton dress drooping at the back, her cardigan hanging limply from her shoulders, and understood her need to be alone. There were times when nothing else was bearable.

Left to herself, Alex found that she had no desire to drive to Furze Hill and picnic on her own. She had left her field diary behind. Now she decided to go back for it and see what material Bridgefield Woods had to offer her for next month's article. Not wishing to disturb Mrs Raynham in her study, for she hated interruptions when she was writing, Alex left the car at the gates and walked round to the side entrance of the house. She could reach her room unheard from there, and would be spared complicated explanations for her return. She fetched her diary, and was walking round the house again when she heard a car draw up, then a car door slammed and footsteps crossed the front terrace. She hesitated, caught a glimpse of Wainwright's grey station wagon, and was about to burst on him with delight when the front door opened and Mrs Raynham stepped out.

"Mr Wainwright?"

Something kept Alex back behind the laurel bush on the corner as he said,

"Yes. And you are Beth's mother. I saw you at Juliet's wedding, Mrs Raynham, but didn't have the pleasure of speaking to you there."

"It was such a crush, wasn't it? I'm terribly sorry, Mr Wainwright, but I'm afraid I've a disappointment for you. Beth's gone out with my secretary for a picnic."

"But . . . You told her I was coming, Mrs Raynham, didn't you?"

"Of course. Immediately she arrived home. But she'd arranged this picnic with Alex, and, well . . ."

"I quite understand." His voice was stiff. "I'm sorry I've troubled you."

"Not at all. Forgive me for not asking you in for a cup of tea, but I'm up to my ears in work. Writing. I'm a journalist, as you probably know."

"Yes. I won't detain you, then, Mrs Raynham."

"When do you leave, Mr Wainwright?"

"Early tomorrow morning. That's why I hoped to see Beth today."

"Yes. Too bad. I'm afraid she's an unpredictable girl, my daughter.

"Well, say goodbye to her for me, Mrs Raynham, will you, and give her my best wishes.

"I certainly will."

The door had closed and Wainwright had driven off before Alex could recover from the shock of Mrs Raynham's duplicity. She had always admired her, in spite of recognising her failure with Beth, which she had put down to lack of sensitivity. Her gaiety and kindness and generosity had shed a light over that house. To find that it was the adornment of a self-love so absolute that her daughter's happiness counted for nothing beside her convenience left Alex gasping. She remembered Nigel's remarks about Beth and her mother. She had repudiated them with scorn. Now she knew that they were true.

Back in the car, she drove towards Bridgefield Woods, but

drew up half-way, unable to concentrate on nature or driving. What should she do? Tell Beth. But how would Beth react? A quarrel with her mother? Mrs Raynham would handle that all right. Some way of glossing it over would be found, and a little hint about Beth's habit of embarrassing men would drive the girl back into herself. One thing was certain. Beth would never approach Peter herself and tell him. The injury inflicted by the Marksman affair had never healed. And what were Peter's feelings for Beth? Just casual friendship? It all hinged on that, and Alex had nothing to go on.

The problem went round and round in her mind. Knowing her own reputation for plunging into things without thought and causing trouble by her impetuosity, she tried hard to keep her anger with Mrs Raynham and her pity for Beth from swamping her reason. But in the end she knew that she would have to act, because Beth was quite incapable of acting on her own behalf, and even if her intervention achieved nothing but trouble, she could not stand by and do nothing while a possible chance of happiness for Beth slipped by. Whatever came of it, she would go to see Wainwright herself that evening. From the moment of that decision, everything seemed to conspire to make it difficult to carry out.

She drove back to the common to see if she could see Beth, and sat in the car, waiting, until it was getting close to dinner-time. She had just decided that Beth must have gone home another way when she saw her walking slowly towards the road, head down, limping a little. Jumping out of the car to meet her, Alex failed to notice the ditch beneath the long grass and stumbled when one leg went down it, wrenching her knee. She stood there, testing it gingerly, while Beth came nearer, still oblivious. She did not see Alex until she was within a few yards, when she smiled wanly and hurried forward. Her smile faded as she saw Alex rubbing her leg.

"What is it, Alex? Have you hurt yourself?"

"Not much. Twisted my knee when I put a leg down that ditch. It's all right. It works. What are you limping for?"

"Was I? Oh, a blister on my heel. Heavens, look at the

time! Thank goodness you came to meet me, Alex. It's only cold dinner tonight, but Mother will be in a flap if we're late, because she's going to that bridge party."

"So she is. Hop in. I think we'll leave her to assume that we've spent the afternoon together, don't you? It will save explanations."

They need not have worried, for Mrs Raynham was absorbed in dressing for the bridge party by the time they arrived home, a long ritual, and she made only the most casual enquiry about their afternoon.

"A pity about your knee, Alex dear," she said. "I was hoping you would have been an angel and driven me over to the Lovats. I hate driving, and Jim Lovat would have driven me home."

"I'm sorry, but I'm afraid it would be difficult. I had a job to drive back this evening, and it's stiffening up now."

"Of course. I wouldn't dream of asking you. Must say I do miss Bruce as a chauffeur. Not that you don't fill the role admirably, Alex, but I feel I shouldn't impose on you too much."

She smiled dazzlingly, and Alex, who had fulfilled the role of car driver just as often as Mrs Raynham wished, murmured that she liked driving, and it was never any trouble.

"Well, I must drive myself, that's all. It's not far. Too bad that Leonard is so seldom home to go with me. But he works so hard, poor sweet, that we can't expect him to endure that tiresome train journey to Bridgefield every night, and his club is so comfortable and convenient."

She refused coffee, and said goodbye, making an attractive picture in a coral silk dress with a little grey squirrel cape round her shoulders.

And just how, Alex wondered, was she to get to Peter Wainwright's cottage with no car and a wrenched knee? The two girls washed the dishes in silence. Beth looked tired to death, her face dull with an apathy that seemed worse than violent unhappiness. It was an acceptance of hopelessness that made Alex more determined than ever to do something about

The pain of her leg as she hobbled round the house made it clear that the half-hour's walk to Bathurst Nurseries was beyond her. Beth usually went there on her bicycle, for the bus offered little help. There remained only Nigel. If she told him the whole story, would he drive her over? He was against interference in other people's lives, but he sympathised with Beth's position in the family and she thought he might help. The trouble was, he was not in a very co-operative mood towards her just then.

"I think I shall go to bed, Alex," said Beth listlessly. "I feel tired."

"Righto. I'll just potter round. Hobble out with Bella, I dare say."

Ben was in the drive, putting the last touches to polishing the car. It was nearly dark when Alex limped up to him.

"Hullo, Ben. Is his lordship in residence?"

"No, Miss Madison. He's spending the evening with Colonel Barry up at Brendon House. A sort of farewell visit, you might say. The Colonel will miss him when we go. A peppery old boy, but they seem to get on well together."

"I wonder if Nigel would mind if I borrowed his car for an hour?"

"I couldn't say, miss. I think he might object. He's rather particular about his car."

Alex thought he might object, too.

"I could telephone him and ask."

"You could, Miss Madison, but he might not like to be interrupted. He and the Colonel enjoy a game of chess as a rule when they're together for a whole evening."

Bother Nigel and his lordly likes and dislikes, thought Alex impatiently. Beth was in trouble and needed help.

"He needn't know about it, Ben."

"Oh no, miss, I couldn't agree to that."

"Well, I'll have to telephone him, then. It's urgent, and I only want it for half an hour. Just to go to the other side of the church. If I hadn't hurt my leg, I could walk it."

As she turned back to the house to telephone, Ben called after her.

"Perhaps I'd better do it, Miss Madison. Wait here."

Alex's eyes gleamed. He obviously didn't trust her to give him Nigel's true reply. And it was that distrust on Ben's part that decided her. She assumed a bland expression which would have warned him had he known her better.

"Thanks, Ben. Tell him it's really important, or I wouldn't ask."

Out of the corner of her eye she had seen the car keys in position, ready for Ben to drive the car back into the garage. As soon as he had disappeared inside the lodge, she slid into the driving seat. She gave a toot on the horn as she drove past the lodge, and when Ben ran out, she was accelerating down the lane.

Chapter Sixteen

ALEX stood among a litter of boxes and suitcases and looked across at the burly figure of Peter Wainwright a little helplessly. She didn't know how to start. He seemed to sense her uneasiness, for he said kindly, waving his pipe at the confusion around them,

"Forgive all this, but I'm making an early start in the morning. Want to get ahead of the removal men. This is the stuff I'm taking myself. I was just going to load it up." He swept a pile of clothes off the couch. "Please sit down."

"I expect you wonder why I've come, and I find it hard to know how to start. You see, I must know how you feel about something before I can start, and I know you'll think I'm impertinent for asking you."

"Asking me what?"

"Would you tell me if it was important to you to see Beth to say goodbye today?"

He looked at her intently, then tapped his pipe out on an ash tray.

"As a matter of fact it was, though I don't see . . . What do you want with me?"

"Oh dear, this is dreadfully difficult."

"Look, I'm a plain man, Miss Madison, and I advise you to be plain with me, too."

"What did you think when you learned that Beth was out this afternoon?"

"That she didn't want to see me, of course. What else? I wasn't altogether surprised, though I'd hoped to find her there."

"Why weren't you surprised?"

"I don't think I'm going to answer any more of this catechism."

"Please, Mr Wainwright, I'm speaking as Beth's friend. Her only friend, except you. There are things you don't know about this afternoon. Beth wasn't given your message. She didn't know you were coming. Her mother told her that you'd telephoned to say goodbye."

"Good heavens! Why on earth should she do that?"

"I can't wash all this dirty linen in front of you unless I know that you care enough for Beth's friendship to want to go on with it, even though you're moving away."

"I do. I was going to ask her to marry me. Now tell me."

She told him of Beth's position at Pelham House, of the Harry Marksman affair and its effect on Beth's almost pathological lack of confidence.

"I see. The bitch," he said slowly, then collected himself. "I'm sorry. You think Beth would have been there for me if she'd known?"

"Wild horses wouldn't have dragged her away."

"I understand now a lot of what has puzzled me about her. Sometimes, she's seemed so close to me, and naturally so, without being conscious of it. And then she'd shy away and be abrupt. And all last week, after I'd told her I was going, she kept away. I assumed that I'd nothing to offer her that she wanted."

"If you only knew how much you have to offer her!"

"Thanks for the compliment, but I'm forty, you know, and

I've not much to show for it. Beth comes from a wealthy home, and I can only provide a very modest kind of set-up. Not that I ever thought that would count much with a young woman like Beth, but still, you never know, and I'm not exactly the answer to a young girl's romantic dreams. I offer hard work and not a lot of money, and I'm middle-aged and set in my ways. I thought we fitted in well, though. She's really interested in my work."

"I don't want to interfere in any way, Mr Wainwright. I only wanted you to know the truth about Beth. The rest is up to you."

"I shall have to tread carefully, shan't I?"

"Yes. I'm so glad you see that. It won't be because she doesn't care, but because she's afraid to believe it, afraid of humiliation again. That's why I don't want her to know I came to you. She'll think I've engineered it, forced you into an embarrassing situation. You don't know how deeply that morbid conviction has bitten into her."

"Or been branded into her. Leave it to me, Miss Madison. I'm more grateful than I can say for your intervention. I shouldn't have tried again. I was sure she didn't want me."

"This evening is just between ourselves, then?"

"Cross my heart. I'll leave here a bit later tomorrow, after all. Will Beth be at home tomorrow morning at half-past nine?"

"Yes. She'll be washing the breakfast dishes, and I shall be in the study with Mrs Raynham, starting on the day's work. If I were you, I'd go to the side entrance."

"I will."

He walked to the door with her, and she said, as he opened it,

"You will remember that Beth's not a very tough character, won't you? She's been undermined by her family and her own diffident nature, so you'll have to be strong for her, and make sure of her."

"You can safely leave that to me," he said, smiling, and Alex knew that she could. He was a man, not a boy, and he would know how to handle Mrs Raynham and any other opposition. He put a hand on her shoulder as he said goodbye.

"You're a good friend to Beth, my dear. However poor a bet I am, I'm a sight better than her family, that's clear. You must come and see us after we're married. Not a bad little house in Kent, and lovely country around. Beth will enjoy herself helping me with the Nurseries, I guess."

"She'll be truly happy for the first time in her life. I'll certainly be there to see it."

Driving back in a glow of elation which helped to soften the pain in her leg, it was not until she turned in by the lodge that she remembered that a certain party would need placating. It was not yet ten, however, and with any luck, he would not have arrived home, in which case the moment of reckoning would be postponed until the following evening. By then, his first wrath would have softened, and affairs of the day would have put her small loan back into perspective. It was possible, too, that he had agreed to it when Ben telephoned him. Comforting herself thus, she drove the car quietly into the garage and left it there. Ben did not come out. He was probably looking at television, and had not heard the car. Her leg was now protesting loudly, and she went straight to bed, thankful to have it off the ground, and well satisfied with her evening's work.

She found it difficult to concentrate on work the next morning. From her own office window, she saw Wainwright's station wagon draw up, but Mrs Raynham's study was at the back of the house, and from there his arrival would be unseen. The first letter which Mrs Raynham dictated was a gracious acceptance of an invitation to speak at the next Women's Institute meeting on Colour in the Home, but Alex's imagination kept straying to the kitchen. It was a good hour before Beth knocked at the door and came in, leading Peter Wainwright by the hand. Her face was bemused with happiness and, for the first time in Alex's experience, she came in without hovering or apologising.

"Mother, I've some wonderful news. I'm going to marry Peter."

That simple statement seemed all that was necessary to Beth. It was left to Wainwright to come forward and add,

"You look surprised, Mrs Raynham, but believe me, it's no sudden thing, really. Beth and I have been close friends since her sister's wedding, so I hope you'll give us your blessing."

"I'm . . . You take my breath away, darling. . . . Of course, I'm delighted," added Mrs Raynham, recovering herself with a rapidity which Alex could not but admire. Her smile was warm and gracious as she held out her hand to Wainwright, but her eyes asked him a question as she said, "Congratulations."

"Thank you. I'm a lucky man, I know. I've been trying to screw up my courage for some time, but like a fool, left it to the last minute and could have kicked myself when Beth was out yesterday. My own fault for assuming she was always here. I simply had to know whether she would marry me before I left Bridgefield, though. Couldn't put my mind to anything else until I knew. You see, my hopes were not all that high."

"Peter, how could you have any doubts?" asked Beth.

"I've told you, my dear. There were lots of reasons why you could think it a pretty poor prospect."

She shook her head, smiling, and tucked her hand under his arm as she said,

"We shall have a very short engagement, Mother. Peter has nobody to look after him in his new home, and domestic help is unknown in the country there. He needs me. We shall be married in a month's time."

"But, darling, what about us?" asked her mother.

"You have Mrs Holloway for most of the cleaning, and I'll see if I can find a cook, though it won't be easy."

"It will be impossible."

"I'm afraid I can't solve that problem for you, Mother. Peter will have nobody at all to look after him, and a new business to establish."

Alex's eyes met Peter's and she smiled her approval. He had done it. No other line of appeal would have drawn Beth to him more surely and speedily than one of need. Service was in her blood. Having established his prior claim, she was his instantly and unswervingly. In fact, if he indicated that he had no clean shirts to wear, Alex believed Beth would down tools instantly at Pelham House and go forthwith to Kent to wash shirts.

"It's no use, Mrs Raynham," said Alex gaily, "we've lost her, and we'll have to face it. She's a wonderful cook, Peter. Your indigestion will vanish in a week."

"Peter, has it been bad again?" asked Beth, concern in her soft eyes.

"A bit grumpy."

"It's all that warmed-up food Mrs Bird gave you. She was the worst housekeeper I've ever come across."

Alex had to admit that Mrs Raynham, when she recognised defeat, accepted it charmingly. She embraced Beth now, and put a hand on Wainwright's shoulder as she said,

"Let's have some sherry, and drink to your happiness, my dears. You're a villain for stealing her so cleverly from under our noses, Peter, but I forgive you."

"I'll look after her well, Mrs Raynham, I promise you," he said, and he smiled at his future mother-in-law with a little mockery in his voice and steady eyes which she met coolly.

"I'm sure you will. I can see you are the solid, reliable type."

She managed to make it sound as though he reminded her of a cart-horse, but that polite little duel between them was quite lost on Beth.

After they had toasted the couple, Wainwright made his excuses for leaving, and Beth went off with him.

"Well," said Mrs Raynham, sinking back into her chair behind her desk. "That's one out of the blue, if you like."

"Yes. I'm glad. He's a nice person, and so right for Beth."

"You didn't think there was anything in it, did you?"

Alex's face was guileless as she shook her head.

"I'm not good at judging such affairs. How happy Beth looked! Sharing his interest in horticulture is going to make it such fun for her."

"Well, everyone to their taste. Digging and weeding and

living in gum boots may be some people's idea of a happy life, but it's not mine, and he would bore me stiff in ten minutes. Still, Beth's made it at last, and one must admit that the choice open to her has never been large. Now, what can we do about replacing her?"

Mrs Raynham tapped her teeth with her pencil reflectively, and was silent for a few moments. Alex said nothing, being too angry with this glimpse of the feline claws usually so well concealed inside their furry sheaths. She spoke of Beth as of a servant.

"Well, let's get on, Alex. We'll have to tackle Beth's little bombshell later."

* * *

Alex's heart sank when Nigel came out of the lodge that evening.

"I want a word with you."

"Will it do after Bella's had her walk?"

"No."

"Then perhaps you'd like to walk with us," suggested Alex sweetly, annoyed at his icy manner.

He looked down at her, and, in the pale light from the porch of the lodge, his face looked unusually grim and sinister. She thought again of Sherlock Holmes, and stooped suddenly to put on Bella's lead, fearing that her untimely sense of humour would be apparent. He appeared to make a visible effort to control himself.

"When you've had your walk, perhaps you'll be good enough to spare me a few minutes inside."

"Very well," said Alex, feeling that she had suddenly slipped back to her schooldays. There were times when Nigel's stilts were absurd.

The air in the lane was sharp with the pungent scent of autumn. Compounded of moist earth, toadstools, dew-wet grass and leaves, it defied description but was instantly recognisable as the end of summer. A sickle-shaped moon was poised on its back in the clear sky like a fragile canoe. A vague feeling of melancholy seized Alex as she walked slowly along, keeping an eye on the snail-slow Bella. Next week, Nigel would be moving to his new house. In a month's time, Beth would be married. Once again, she was experiencing the sense of desertion she had known at home, when, one by one, companions left her until she was alone, peering out of the window at departing figures like a dog left behind. She hoped Nigel would not be too angry with her. She felt forlorn and in need of comfort.

Comfort, however, was as far from Nigel's face as the Riviera from the North Pole, when he invited her into his sitting-room.

"You didn't like me borrowing your car?" she asked, plunging into the deep end without preamble.

"I did not."

"You refused when Ben asked you, I suppose?"

"Yes."

"And he told you I'd taken it."

"I saw you driving it home. I was walking down Colonel Barry's drive when you passed. What damned impudence, Alex! You seem to think anything is yours for the taking."

"I'm sorry, Nigel, but it really was important. Your mother was using her car, and I only wanted to go a little way, but I'd twisted my knee and couldn't walk far. It still hurts a bit."

"Then you'd better sit down," he said grimly, indicating the armchair behind her.

"Well, don't loom over me. I've said I'm sorry. It was important, and I had to get transport."

"Perhaps you'll be kind enough to tell me what this important mission was," he said, sitting down in the armchair opposite her and taking out his cigarette-case.

"If you'll promise me not to mention it ever to anyone."

"You're not imposing the terms at this interview, my girl. I am."

"Then I shan't tell you."

"Good grief, if you're not enough to try the patience of a saint! All right. I'll not talk."

She told him about Wainwright and Beth.

"And this morning, he asked her to marry him and she

accepted. Isn't that splendid? You must admit that I borrowed your car in a good cause."

"How do you know it's splendid? Is matrimony bound to be an improvement on the single state? This chap may be a brute, for all you know."

"He's a good, kind person. I liked him as soon as I spoke to him."

"One of your infallible intuitions?" he asked dryly.

"I didn't interfere, Nigel. I only put right your mother's misrepresentation. If you had seen them together this morning, you could have no doubt. At least, you might. You seem to cherish doubts as other people cherish pets," she said, growing angry.

"I use my mind, not my emotions."

"Then use your mind now. They share the same interests. He's a nurseryman."

"Does that make him a good husband? Beth's not a cabbage."

"People who work with growing, living things, whether plants or animals, are far more likely to be good people than those who deal with dead things like chemicals and commodities. Contact with nature in any form has a humanising effect. Your work seems to have dehumanised you."

"Very likely. But is your judgment always so sound?"

"In this case it is. And that was spiteful."

He was looking up at the spiral of smoke trailing above his head and made no reply. Alex waited a moment, then said desperately,

"Think what Beth's life is now, and what she will be like if she stays at Pelham House as a servant for the rest of her days. That's all she is. The others don't give two pins for her. They've just used her. You were right about the family. Now she's escaping to a home of her own and a man who's seen the real Beth underneath that awkward exterior. You condemn him without ever having seen him, just because you're angry with me for taking your car. I think it did good work last night, and I'm not even sorry. I'd do it again. Some things are more important than getting permission. You wouldn't have minded if it had been a case of saving a life. Well, this was."

"You're very vehement." He suddenly looked tired and drawn, and anger had drained away from him. "All right, Alex. You win. That simplicity of yours is a devastating weapon. You pole-axe me with it. Forget it. But I'd sooner you did the explaining first and the borrowing after, in future."

"I don't suppose I'll have much chance to borrow anything in the future. I shall miss you, Nigel. I hope you'll let me come and see your house when you're in."

"Invade my peace there as you've invaded it here?" he asked, with a crooked grin.

"Have I really been a nuisance?"

"A very disturbing influence on the atmosphere, shall we say?"

"Oh, well, that's life. It can't always go along in just the calm way you'd like. Beth and Peter are getting married next month. Your mother's going to be in a fix."

"There is no fix that my mother cannot ease her way out of, babe. I'm sorry if I've been a bit gritty lately. Put it down to liver."

"I thought you were still angry with me about . . . Jane."

"That was outrageous, but no, it wasn't that."

"I expect it's the move. One foot here and one foot there. It's a bit trying for you, fitting it in with such a demanding job."

"You're being very soothing. I shall begin to think you want to borrow something again."

"I don't want to quarrel again with you before you go. We seem to have done a good deal of quarrelling, one way and another. That's odd, really. I haven't quarrelled with the others, and yet . . ."

"And yet?"

"I was going to say, you're the only reliable one here."

"Reliable for what? Quarrelling?"

"Not being different underneath from what's on top."

"That certainly simplifies things," he said, half smiling,

then added, "Like a cup of coffee? I'm going to have one before I start a spot of work."

While he went out to the kitchen, she picked up a business magazine and leafed through it. She stopped at a photograph of Nigel. A very good one, she thought. Underneath, she read, "Dr Nigel Lynton, who next month becomes Head of our Research Station on the retirement of Dr Thornley."

He brought the tray of coffee and put it on the table beside her, saying,

"You pour."

"Congratulations, Nigel. Why didn't you tell us?" she asked, indicating the photograph.

"Didn't think of it, babe."

She could well believe it. He was singularly independent. It would not be modesty that kept him from making it known, but a complete detachment from the approval or disapproval of other people. More than anybody she knew, he was self-sufficient, a free man. She both admired him for it and was exasperated by it. That night, however, it caused her a dull little ache inside. Watching him as he sipped his coffee, she realised fully for the first time just how much she was going to miss him.

Chapter Seventeen

ALEX went home a little reluctantly the following week-end, for it was the last one which Nigel would be spending at the lodge, but it was also her god-daughter's first birthday on Saturday, and she had promised to be home for the party. On the Friday evening, she put out tentative feelers to see if he would like to come to Camerino with her.

"It's rather a lovely old house," she said, leaning on the gate of the lodge. "I think you'd find it interesting."

"Afraid I'm too busy clearing up here this week-end, babe, but thanks all the same."

"Another time, perhaps," she said, then added hastily, "I don't suppose you'd have enoyed this week-end party, anyway. My sisters are coming home, and we're all trooping over to Clive's tomorrow for Elizabeth's first birthday. I expect children are your pet aversion, and David, that's Clive's son, is a little terror."

"Does Clive live near your home, then?"

"Only ten minutes in the car. Dad depends on him a lot to help run the estate, so Clive felt he had to live fairly close. We grow timber. I believe I told you."

"Yes. Clive has a business of his own in Elton, too, hasn't he? At least, if he's the Madison Guy deals with. They make doors and pulpits and altar screens. Quality stuff."

"That's right."

"Then I'm a customer. His firm supplied my front door and front gates."

"Well, what do you know? That makes a link. You'll be able to think of me every time you close the door. A Madison door."

"You're a closely knit family, by the sound of it."

"Yes, I suppose we are. I don't think I'd realised it until I discovered how different the family life is here."

"In what way?"

"They all pursue their own ends, almost oblivious of each other under the surface. I suppose that's better than interfering and damaging each other, but lately the wind blowing through Pelham House has seemed a bit chilling. It's so right on top, and so wrong underneath. At home, we don't interfere with each other, but we do care. We are interested."

"You know, I think you'd do well to go back home and look for another job. It'll be lonely for you here after Beth goes, and I bet Mother will try to make a housekeeper of you as well as a secretary unless she can find someone to take Beth's place."

"There's something about me," said Alex gloomily. "I always seem to get left behind."

"Cheer up. What about that career in journalism you told me you were pursuing so ardently?"

"I know. Guess I'm feeling a bit unsettled, that's all. I love my work for Mr Barling." She broke off and laid a hand on his arm. "Look. Up that hazel tree. A grey squirrel. Collecting nuts for the winter. Isn't he graceful? There he goes."

"Where?"

"He's reached the beech tree behind."

She ran out to the lane to watch the squirrel's rapid flight across the tree tops. When she returned to the lodge, Nigel was opening the front door.

"So long, babe."

"So long. When are you moving, Nigel?"

"Tuesday."

"Want any help in packing up?"

"No, thanks. Ben will cope."

He waved a hand and the door closed behind him. Alex walked slowly up the drive to the house. Somehow, the closing of that door seemed depressingly significant.

She cheered up a little at the family gathering that weekend. It was pleasant to be with her sisters again, and to be back in the old teasing, friendly give-and-take atmosphere. Better still, to have Sarah to herself for a whole hour before the party began on Saturday, while Elizabeth slept and Clive took David out for a walk. It was not until she was walking alone round the garden of Camerino after tea on Sunday that the melancholy mood stole over her again. Happy as they all were to see her, they had lives that absorbed them. Rosalind was expecting a baby in the spring, Delia had already rushed back to her hotel, where the season was at its height, and Sarah and Clive had their home and children. You came back, but life had moved on, and it was never quite the same again. She had moved on, too, but just now she could not see ahead. Nigel loomed too large. Her heart felt as though it was going through a mangle when she thought of the lodge, empty and waiting for new tenants. Mrs Raynham was holding it out as a bait for a couple to act as housekeeper and gardener, but so far, there had been no applicants.

As she came to the woodland garden, she noticed two stone urns beside a rhododendron bush. They were the two which used to stand at the entrance to the sunken rose garden, and it occurred to her that they would be exactly right for the top of the steps from Nigel's terrace. They were a lovely classical shape, mossy and weathered. He should have them. They were obviously not wanted here, for in their place above the rose garden stood two lead figures. With Alex, no sooner was the thought in her mind than action followed. Her father was not to be found, but her mother was talking baby talk with Rosalind.

"Can I borrow the car, Mother? I just want to slip over to my friend's new house with those two old urns we've finished with. It won't take more than an hour. I'll be back to supper."

"All right, darling," said her mother absent-mindedly. "Your father's taking Ian round the estate, so we shan't have supper until half-past eight. Take care."

Baby talk had been rather too dominant this week-end, Alex decided. Odd that her mother, always so sensible about her own children, should have become so sentimental about her grandchildren. The urns were heavy, and it took her some time to roll them down the garden and hoist them into the back of the car. She half hoped that Nigel would be at the house, but it was deserted when she arrived. It looked very elegant and inviting in the mellow light of the setting sun. Already the landscape gardeners had worked miracles since she had last seen it. When the newly planted trees in the front had matured, and the young climber on the front of the house had reached the grey timbering, it would make a most attractive picture. She was glad they had planted wistaria. Its lavender blue flowers would show up beautifully against the pale grey timbering. Wistfully, she wondered whether she would ever see it bloom. She was under no illusion about Nigel's complete independence, and did not expect he would take steps to see her often, if at all, in the future. The name was now on the gate. Marchwood.

With difficulty, she manipulated the urns round to the terrace along the back of the house. Mellow stone had been used for this, and the urns sat on it, one at each side of the flight of steps down to the lawn, as though they had grown there. She knew that Nigel had been ferreting round unsuccessfully for something to stand there. He was terribly fussy, but she thought that even his critical eye would see that these were right. She would tell him in the morning. Meanwhile, it comforted her to have left a little bit of herself in the garden of Nigel's new home. Such a sentimental feeling shocked her, however. Really, she was as bad as her mother with the babies. Odd, that one had these melting, treacly moments.

Back at Pelham House next day, Alex waited impatiently for Nigel to return in the evening so that she could tell him about the urns. He had not arrived before dinner, and she strolled down to the lodge afterwards, presuming that he had arrived meanwhile. Ben opened the door.

"Is Nigel available, Ben, or is he in the middle of his dinner?"

"He's not coming home tonight, Miss Madison. Had a conference to attend at Head Office in London, and he's staying in town for the evening. Going to the opera, I think he said."

"Going to the opera on the evening before he moves?"

"Yes. There's nothing to do here. We're leaving everything to the removal men now. We packed up personal things, papers, and so on, this week-end and the rest can be tackled by the men."

"I see. Will he be coming back here tomorrow morning?"

"No. Going straight to the Research Station. He's left his car at Elton Station. He always does that when he goes up to London. It's a fast service from Elton."

"Yes, I know. He's said goodbye to the lodge, then."

"Yes, Miss. We'll be in our new residence tomorrow. Can't say I'll be sorry. A bit unsettling, knowing you're going to move. Makes you lose interest in a place."

"Yes," said Alex, stunned by Nigel's sudden exit.

"If you'll excuse me, Miss Madison, I'll just dump this sack of paper out here for the dustman to take for salvage."

He propped the bulging sack against the dustbin and returned to the lodge, rubbing his hands.

"Well, that's that. A fine clear-out we've had."

Alex said goodbye to him, and turned away. A magazine had slipped out of the sack on to the ground and she went to pick it up. It was the magazine she had looked at the previous week. She took it back to the house with her. In her bedroom, she cut out the photograph of Nigel, and sat on her bed looking at it, still finding it hard to believe that he had gone without saying goodbye to her. Perhaps it meant that he would be getting in touch with her, but she drew little comfort from this slender hope. For weeks past now, she had sensed his withdrawal. Nothing obvious, but a subtle disengagement, as though other pressing affairs, business and his new home, left no space for her any longer. She sat there for a long time, stiff and cold, hugging herself tightly as though holding herself together, looking into an empty future.

She waited two weeks for him to get in touch with her, but heard nothing. At last, thinking of him one evening when she was writing up her field diary, she decided to write him a letter. It took a surprisingly long time to compose.

DEAR NIGEL,

I hope you liked the urns. I thought they were just what you wanted when I saw them in the garden at home, so I popped over with them. Of course, if you don't like them, I shan't be at all offended. Just meant for a small contribution to your new home, which I think is lovely, and a thank-you for your guidance when I first came to Pelham House. I know I didn't take it very well, but I appreciate your kindness now when I look back. Anyway, throw them out if you don't like them.

The lodge is still empty, and we haven't had a single application for the job of housekeeper.

Hope Marchwood is as nice to live in as it is to look at.

Yours,

ALEX

When she read it through, it seemed too obvious a bid for an invitation to Marchwood. He would get in touch with her if he wanted to. If not, there was little point in sending that letter. As she hesitated, there was a knock at the door and Beth came in. Alex slipped the letter into her diary, and welcomed her with a smile.

"Well, how was Peter? Starved and poking out at the elbows?"

"Not exactly, but all this travelling between there and home has kept me so busy that I've had no time to buy my wedding outfit yet. That's what I wanted to ask you, Alex. Will you come to Elton with me tomorrow to see what we can find? Mother says you can have the day off, because she's going to London."

"Of course. I'd like to."

"I prefer to have someone with me for support. Otherwise I find a pressing assistant lands me with something I hate."

"Well, with less than a week to your wedding day, Beth, you're certainly cutting it fine."

"There are more important things in life than clothes, and they're rather wasted on me, anyway."

She spoke quite happily, as though the fact did not worry her at all, and Alex marvelled at the quiet confidence which had flowed into Beth since Peter had asked her to marry him. That she loved him devotedly, there could be no doubt, and she had displayed the energy of an Amazon in dividing her life between the cottage in Kent and Pelham House. In contrast to the furore that had reigned for weeks before Juliet's wedding, Beth's was causing little comment or action on her mother's part. In fact, Alex believed that, having written Beth off as housekeeper, Mrs Raynham gave her very little thought at all, and had not yet been to see the cottage, although Beth had twice asked her. The wedding, at Beth's request, was to be a very quiet one, with no guests outside the family, and it had been left to Alex to make what arrangements were necessary.

They enjoyed their day in Elton, and bought a dove-grey suit for Beth. It took some time to find the right hat, and in the course of their explorations, Alex bought a small floral concoction for herself. By the time Beth had ordered more table linen and curtain material, the day was almost over, and they returned, tired but triumphant, just ahead of Mrs Raynham. As soon as Alex saw Mrs Raynham's face, she knew that something had happened to please her.

"Don't tell me," she said. "You've found a housekeeper."

"No. Better still. I've found a perfectly lovely flat close to Regent's Park. It solves all my problems. Service on the premises, every luxury you can think of, easy, gracious living at last. I've finished with the country, Alex. We shall be moving there in December."

Beth was upstairs, unpacking her parcels, and Alex sank down into the nearest chair in the drawing-room while Mrs Raynham went on.

"I've been scouting round for a week or two now, ever since it became apparent that a housekeeper wasn't going to materialise, and I was tipped off about this flat by a friend. An end to all this tedious travelling up and down to London. We can entertain our friends so much more easily in London, and it will be very convenient for my husband," she added as an afterthought.

"Yes, I suppose it will," said Alex, a little bewildered.

"I'm not really a countrywoman, you know, dear. Not even the sort of hybrid woman who can keep one foot in London and one in the country. London is my spiritual and intellectual home. I was foolish to think I could ever be really happy anywhere else. My friends all told me I should be stifled in this parochial atmosphere, and they were right. Of course, I only did it for the children. But now they've all gone, Leonard and I can just please ourselves."

Never, thought Alex, had she been concerned with pleasing anybody but herself.

"But you, Alex, dear. You're such a treasure. Dare I hope that you would come to London with us?"

"I'm afraid not, Mrs Raynham. I love the country. I shouldn't want to live in London."

"Oh dear! What a shame! I was afraid not. But you will stay with me until we move, dear, won't you? I simply can't do without you while I'm clearing up at this end and supervising at the other." She saw the hesitation on Alex's face and plunged on, holding out her hands appealingly. "I shall hate losing you, dear. You've been the greatest help, and are the sweetest person. I'm very, very fond of you. And I shall insist on your coming to stay with us, and being a frequent visitor. You will, dear, won't you?"

"Of course, if I'm asked," said Alex, smiling in spite of herself at this lavish display of charm.

"You will be the first to be asked. The very first. And you will stay on here until we move, won't you? Don't leave me in the lurch, as all the others have done."

It was difficult to resist Mrs Raynham's appeal, although Alex could see little to attract her in the prospect of staying on at Pelham House as general dogsbody until the Raynhams moved to their luxury flat. But, smilingly, she agreed. After all, Mrs Raynham had been kind to her.

"Bless you, dear. I knew I could rely on you. So loyal. A real stalwart in a world of reeds. Hullo, Beth."

Beth had come running down the stairs, her new suit over her arm.

"Look, Mother. Do you like it? My wedding suit."

"Yes, dear. Very nice. Beth, I've some news. I found a flat in London today. A service flat, with the most heavenly rooms. Spacious, with huge windows. I've decided that we'll go there to live, your father and I."

"That sounds a sensible solution," said Beth quietly.

"Yes. What do we want with this big house now that you children have gone? We can live a really civilised life there, with all that London offers right on our doorstep. I shall give up my work for *Downland Journal*, of course. I was always wasted on that, anyway. Too old-fashioned in outlook. Might be a good idea to contact one or two of my old editors."

She ran on, making her plans, excited and absorbed. The two girls were not called upon to comment. After a little, Beth slipped away, her suit still over her arm.

"Of course, the rent is fabulous. But we ought to get a good price for this house, and, after all, Leonard is a rich man. This flat will provide just the right background for him."

"Does Mr Raynham know anything about it yet?"

"No, dear. I shall tell him tonight. He knows I've had it in mind to move back to London, of course. He'll be delighted that I've found such a lovely flat, once he's got over the shock of the rent. But I've no doubts at all about his agreement."

Nor had Alex. Mrs Raynham was a superb saleswoman and he would agree to anything for the sake of being left alone to get on with his business. She would dispose of any objections he might raise as quickly and easily as she had disposed of Beth's wedding suit, Alex's job and David Barling's journal. Other people's needs penetrated her ego no deeper than specks of dust on a polished wooden table. Alex marvelled, as she sat there, at the power of charm allied to single-minded egoism. It had taken her in completely at first, and could still cast rosy veils before her eyes.

Chapter Eighteen

THE hedge along the lane was already showing the gold and scarlet of autumn's pageant when Alex drove Mrs Raynham to Bridgefield Church for Beth's wedding. A few leaves spun slowly down from the overhanging trees ahead of them, pale gold from the birch, a vivid scarlet from the wayfaring tree.

"The last of the children to go. Who would have thought they would all be married within a year?" observed Mrs Raynham, adjusting her fur stole.

She wore a pale lavender silk suit which quite eclipsed the bride, but Beth's happy face as she waited for her father in the hall at Pelham House had warmed Alex's heart and made it clear that this was Beth's day.

Peter was already waiting beside his best man as Alex joined Nigel, Bruce and his wife in the pew. There was something enormously reassuringly about that broad back of Peter's, she thought. She smiled up at Nigel, who said "Hullo", and raised his eyebrows at her hat. Then Beth came in on her father's arm and the service started. It was a good thing that the church was small, thought Alex, or else the little group of guests would have looked very lonely indeed. There had been a rash of weddings in her life lately. This was the fourth she had attended since her sister's wedding less than a year ago. Very conscious of Nigel's closeness, she hoped he would come back to Pelham House after the luncheon party at a nearby hotel.

He sat next to her at the lunch, and was extremely affable.

"Nice chap, Wainwright. Full marks for your intuition this time, Alex," he said, after they had toasted the bride and groom.

"Thank you. I'm so glad for Beth. It's really quite a Cinderella story, isn't it?"

"Well, I doubt whether Wainwright would qualify for a Prince Charming, but I should say they'll be a good deal happier together than they are apart."

"Rash words, indeed, from such a sceptic," said Alex, laughing up at him.

"That's a nobby little hat. Not used to seeing that hair of yours quenched. By a few primroses, too."

The little helmet of veiling and flowers matched her linen suit and lifted it on to an altogether more frivolous plane, she felt. Not usually much concerned with clothes, she had dressed that morning with special care, and was pleased that he had noticed the hat.

"How are you liking life at Marchwood?"

"It suits me very well indeed, thank you. Mother, I hear, is off to London in December."

"Yes. She can't talk of anything else. I think it's the life for her."

"Yes. And you?"

"I shall be out of work at the end of the year. I'm staying until the move."

"Any plans afterwards?"

"I haven't had time to think about it yet. Beth's wedding has kept me pretty busy for the past few days. Nobody else seemed to be bothering much. I shall go home and vegetate for a bit, I expect. Until after Christmas, anyway. I shall still be one of Mr Barling's contributors, of course."

"You'll have to make a start on that book you said you wanted to write."

She wished he wouldn't talk about her future in such a detached manner. Somehow, it depressed her. She searched her mind for some way of introducing the subject of the urns. It was unlike her to feel diffident about discussing anything with him, but suddenly she felt a little embarrassed by the whole business. While she hesitated, his attention was taken by Eve, on the other side of him, and then it was time for Beth and Peter to leave. They were spending a week in Guernsey for their honeymoon, that being all the time they could spare from the Nurseries, and it was Alex to whom they both turned at the last. Peter, usually an undemonstrative man, gave her a hug as he said,

"Goodbye, dear Alex. We both owe you a lot. You'll come and see us often, won't you?"

Alex knew that this was an invitation which was sincerely meant, and was not a mere polite gesture, for Peter had no time or skill for conventional ploys. She would be visiting the cottage in Kent when Mrs Raynham had forgotten her existence. Beth's arms were round her next, and she said tremulously,

"Goodbye, Alex. Bless you. And thank you for everything. You've been such a help and an example to me."

Before Alex, flabbergasted at this last tribute, could do more than smile and kiss her, Peter had taken his wife's arm, and together they ran down the path to the waiting car. The rest was a decided anti-climax. Juliet and her husband had to hurry back to London for a dinner that evening, Nigel made his excuses and left immediately afterwards, and Bruce and Eve came back to Pelham House only for tea, and then went on to spend the evening with Eve's mother, taking Mrs Raynham with them, for she declared that she needed company that evening. Mr Raynham, inevitably, went to his study to work, and Alex, declining Mrs Raynham's invitation to go with them, was left alone with Bella.

Putting away her wedding hat, she reflected that Nigel had slipped away like a ghost that afternoon, waving to her across the room as he went. Engaged in conversation with Juliet, she could only wave back. By the time she had freed herself and reached the door of the hotel, the Jaguar was nosing its way out of the car park. The primroses on the hat suddenly blurred in front of her eyes, and a tear splashed on to the veiling and lay there like a drop of dew. Hastily wrapping tissue paper over it, she put the lid on the box and placed the box on top of the wardrobe. She would probably never wear it again. There were no more single people in her circle to get married now.

Bella had followed her upstairs, and now sprawled on the rug in front of the cold electric fire, her eyes following Alex's every movement. As she grew older and deafer, and her eyes grew dimmer, Bella seemed to depend more and more on Alex, as though the rest of the world had suddenly grown menacing. Alex stooped and patted her head. There was still Bella to look after.

In the weeks that followed Beth's wedding, Alex seemed to be inhabiting a no-man's-land. With Mrs Raynham spending more time in London than ever, it was left to Alex to show possible purchasers over Pelham House, and they came in a steady stream from the agents until the beginning of November, when the house was sold. With the help of the daily woman, Alex was left to run the house, as well as cope with the correspondence and articles, as before. By the time December came in with blustery wet weather, she was feeling ragged with tiredness, her usual boundless energy worn away. Perhaps it was the dogged unhappiness underlying her work which sapped her vitality more than the chores themselves, for when Jane telephoned one evening to invite her to spend a day there, her tiredness fled at Jane's words.

"Nigel's coming to dinner in the evening, and I thought it would be nice to have a foursome. Can you have the day off, and come to lunch with me? It would make the journey more worth while for you."

"I expect so. Hold on, Jane. I'll find out."

Mrs Raynham was agreeable, as she would be in London that day, and Alex ran back to the telephone as though on wings.

"Yes, Jane. It's all right, and I'd love to. Mrs Raynham says I can borrow her car, so that will make it easy."

When she set off two mornings later, the pouring rain did nothing to depress her. The prospect of seeing Nigel that evening glowed so warmly in her mind that she was invulnerable to weather. As the windscreen wiper clicked monotonously and scarcely fast enough to keep the windscreen clear, she sang a little tune and drove merrily on.

Nigel arrived after Guy that evening, and as he came into the hall and greeted Jane, he did not notice Alex in the doorway of the sitting-room until she came forward with a smile. When he saw her, he stopped in mid-sentence with a look of surprise which told her that he had not known she would be there. Her smile faded at the grim expression which followed his surprise. He recovered himself almost immediately and greeted her with his usual urbane smoothness, but the shock of that reaction left Alex trembling.

She tried to put it out of her mind during dinner, but it lurked there like a snake in shadow, the realisation that Nigel's pleasure at seeing his friends had been spoilt by her appearance. To cover up the shock, she made an extra effort to appear gay, and on the surface, it was a happy little dinner party.

Over coffee, Alex explained, in answer to Nigel's enquiry, that Pelham House had just been sold.

"Completion of the sale is fixed for the week after your mother moves to London, so it's all worked out very well. Must say I was glad when it was sold and I had no more people to show over the house. I began to feel like an attendant at a stately home thrown open to the public," she said.

When she told him the price it had fetched, he whistled.

"Does the lodge go with it?"

"Yes. The new tenants are buying that for the wife's parents to live in."

"It's a good price for a place as large as Pelham House.

The larger the house, the poorer the price, as a rule, these days," said Guy.

"I liked the lodge," said Jane. "I shan't ever forget the night we spent there, though. What a storm!"

"And what a party!" groaned Guy.

Jane's eyes sparkled as she looked across at her husband.

"Well, you'd done your best to duck it, darling."

"You misjudged me, woman. I did not arrange that business trip just because I knew it was the week of your mother's silver wedding party. It just happened like that."

"And then the car broke down, and you had to postpone the business trip after all. I still think there was a little poetic justice in that."

"Don't you like parties, then, Guy?" asked Alex, carefully avoiding Nigel's eye.

"Yes, on the whole. Not this particular one, though. My uncle, who is Jane's step-father, is not our favourite character. In fact, he was very unkind to Jane in the old days, before we were married. He is addicted to giving lavish parties and showing off his wealth to the humbler members of his family group. Jane felt she had to go for her mother's sake. But I really didn't arrange that business trip deliberately. I'd forgotten. I didn't particularly want to throw you back into the family den without my support, Jane."

"I know, darling. I was only teasing. Anyway, Nigel came to the rescue and saved us from having to spend the night there. To offer us both bedroom and the use of your car was real friendship, Nigel."

"You were welcome," said Nigel, grinning, "though I wouldn't have offered the car to anybody but Guy, who is a reasonably good driver. It just happened that I didn't want either bed or car that night. I must confess to being slightly relieved at seeing the Jag waiting for me, intact, at Elton Station next morning, though. Funny how possessive you get about a car."

"I wonder what you get up to after these conferences in London, Nigel?" asked Jane.

"That's telling, sweetheart."

"Anyway, if we'd had to stay the night with Mummy, we'd have been sleeping on the conservatory floor. They were packed out. J.J., that's my step-father," said Jane to Alex, "had allotted the available beds and couches to more favoured members of the family. I think he was disappointed when we explained that we'd been offered accommodation elsewhere."

"Do they live far from Bridgefield?"

"No. Only five or six miles, at Elmhurst."

"Their house is an example of the most shocking architecture it has ever been my misfortune to look upon," said Guy. "Every conceivable style thrown in to make J.J. think he was getting value for his money. Gothic, Regency, Victorian, the lot. It looks like a cross between Prinny's Palace at Brighton and a Spanish castle. If you ever go through Elmhurst, take a look at it, Nigel. It's a stunner."

The talk drifted to architecture and thence to travels abroad, for Jane and Guy usually spent their holidays touring Europe, and Alex was able to relax and listen. The evening which she had longed for with such ardour now seemed an ordeal, for the kindness of Jane and Guy could not wipe out that look on Nigel's face. When she and Nigel were left alone for a few minutes, she did not know what to say. It was the first time that self-consciousness had come between them. Theirs had been an unusually frank relationship from the first. Now, it had all changed, and she could think of no way to restore it. At last she said desperately,

"Guy and Jane have been providing heaps of ashes for my head this evening. That was a shocking howler of mine. I hope you've forgotten it, Nigel."

"Say no more."

Finesse she would never have, she thought, as she blurted out,

"You weren't pleased to see me tonight, were you?"

"I was surprised. Jane hadn't mentioned you."

"Why weren't you pleased? Have I done anything to offend you?"

And at the very moment that she spoke, she saw it all, and her face flushed crimson. Here, in this very room, he had expounded his views on matrimony and the cleverness of woman's pursuit of man. He had been quicker than she to realise that the quality of her friendship had changed; he saw her now as a pursuer. Scarcely knowing what she did, she crossed the room and stood gazing with unseeing eyes at a picture on the wall. Nigel's eyes followed her.

"Nice colouring in that landscape, isn't there?" he observed, ignoring her question.

"Very. I like the sunshine and shadow across the downs."

To Alex's intense relief, Jane came in at that moment, and she was not alone with Nigel again that evening. She left at ten, shaking hands with him and managing a smiling goodbye. It was still raining, and Guy and Jane stood in the porch to see her off. She waved a hand as she drove away, the rain sending silver rods across her headlights. Suitable weather for goodbyes, she thought, dimming her lights as a car approached. She felt numbed after the revelations of that evening, and drove back to Pelham House in a state of cold detachment which surprised her. She felt too weary by the time she reached there to care very much about anything, but once in bed, her mind free to roam, feeling came back to her in a painful flood, and she could not stop the scalding tears.

* * *

"One more thing, dear. My husband telephoned the vet in the village last night and asked him to collect Bella. We've decided that it's time the poor old dog was put down. He'll be here before ten."

Alex, scarcely crediting her ears, repeated,

"Put down?"

"Yes, dear. It's kindest really. And we can't have her in the flat. Oh, I forgot. One more thing. Will you make a hairdressing appointment for me with Mr Berenger at this number?" She pulled a card out of her handbag and gave it to Alex. "I've been strongly recommended to him. He's said to be a wonderful stylist, and his establishment is conveniently close to the flat. The only snag is, you have to book up for weeks in advance, so find out the first morning he can take me, not before ten, and book it. I can work other engagements round it. Oh, and tell them Felicity Barnsley recommended me. The model, you know."

Alex didn't know, and was not interested.

"You can't have Bella put down, Mrs Raynham. She's perfectly healthy and still enjoys life. In fact, since I've had the feeding of her and have exercised her, she's a lot fitter than when I first came."

"I'm sorry, Alex, but Leonard was quite determined about it, and he'll only say we're sentimental if we argue. Anyway, it's quite impossible to have her in London. She was bought for Juliet in the first place, but she doesn't want her. She has two poodles. Such sweet little things, and so intelligent."

"Then can I have Bella? She can come home with me."

"But won't your parents object? She's old and blind, and quite a liability."

"She's not blind and they're used to liabilities," said Alex briefly.

"Very well, dear. If you really want to take Bella, of course you can. You'd better try to catch Elliot before he leaves. Now that really is the lot, I think. How I'm going to get my packing done by tonight, I don't know. Come up and give me a hand when you've finished the letters, dear, will you?"

Alex returned to her office and sat down at her desk, shocked by Mrs Raynham's attitude to Bella. It was not so much the decision to have the old dog destroyed as the casual way she had mentioned it, as though it was a question of dumping rubbish in a dustbin, of small significance beside the booking of a hairdressing appointment with a fashionable London hairdresser. It broke the last link between Alex and her employer.

The vet arrived before Alex could telephone, and Bella was with her in the hall when she opened the door to him.

"I'm sorry, Mr Elliot, but I'm afraid we've brought you on a fruitless journey. I'm going to look after the spaniel. Mrs Raynham has given her to me."

The vet, a tall, thin man whom Alex had met before when he had come to treat Bella for canker, smiled as he stooped to pat the reprieved animal, who wagged her tail ingratiatingly and contrived to look terrified at the same time. He carried a scent which spelt trouble.

"I'm glad to hear it. She's not in bad trim for an old lady. How old is she?"

"Twelve."

He was running his hands over her, inspecting her eyes.

"Good for a couple of years yet, I'd say."

Alex smiled on him warmly.

"That's what I thought. After all, as long as she can still enjoy a walk, and lying in the sun, and eating, I think she's a right to live. I've an old dog at home. They can keep each other company."

He went off, with his ominous black case unopened, and Alex allowed Bella to stay in her office with her to celebrate their new relationship.

Chapter Nineteen

MRS RAYNHAM left on the Friday morning soon after the removal men arrived. Alex was remaining at Pelham House that night in order to supervise the collection of odds and ends of unwanted furniture by a firm of auctioneers the next morning. Meanwhile, she kept clear of the removal men by staying in her room with Bella for most of the day. The furniture there was destined for the auction rooms. Her employer's farewell had been fond and even extravagant in its expression of regret and appreciation, but Alex had remained unmoved, knowing that it was largely an act and that she would have been removed as calmly as Bella had she been in the way. The invitations to come to London were repeated fervently, but would never be translated into anything concrete, thought Alex, who doubted if she would ever see Barbara Raynham again. She had blazed into her life on Rosalind's wedding day, and now sailed away, as charming and superficial and elegant as a toy yacht. Just before leaving, she had pressed a generous cheque into Alex's hand.

It was a wild morning, with a gale-force wind tossing the branches of the birch trees so that they looked tormented as the men worked away in the front drive. It was a melancholy business, watching a house being emptied, Alex thought, as she sat at her bedroom window. She felt tired and dispirited. The wind had roared round the house since the early morning, waking her with its violence, and she had watched the dawn break.

Nigel was supposed to be coming over at lunch-time to collect some books of his father's. Thinking of him, she decided to go down to the study and make sure that the men were not taking them by mistake. She had labelled them, together with all the other items not to be taken, but her faith in men was not so high that she entirely trusted them to use their eyes. These books were valuable, and when Nigel had enquired after them and learned that they were for the auction rooms, too, he had claimed them, since they had belonged to his father. She had not seen him, as these arrangements had been made with his mother by telephone. Now, she viewed his visit with confusion, torn between the joy which she would always feel at the sight of him and pain at his rejection of her.

Having established that the books had been safely left in splendid isolation in the study, she went to the kitchen and made tea for the men. They worked quickly and efficiently, with a good deal of noise, and at three o'clock the van moved off, and Alex was left alone. Of Nigel, there had been no sign. The almost empty rooms echoed dismally as she walked through them. It was going to be a miserable business, staying here until the next day. She would be glad to be back at Camerino.

She jumped at the sound of wood tearing away outside the dining-room window. It was a large branch from one of the birch trees, torn from the main trunk and hanging suspended by a thin strip. As she watched, the wind seized it and tore it free. It was a savage, frenzied wind, and she was tired of its noisy destructiveness. Dead leaves were whirling over the lawn like things demented, and a sheet of newspaper sailed past the window and wrapped itself round the trunk of a tree as though pasted there. The cypress tree beyond the lodge was arched over by the onslaught of the wind until it must surely break, she thought. Then she saw the kitten. A small black and white object, its fur blown on end, crouched under the hedge. She went out to it, bending almost double against the fury of the wind, and it half ran, was half blown towards her. Its back legs and tail were wet, but the rest was dry and fluffy, and vibrated with a purr as Alex nestled it against her sweater. It was one of the litter recently produced by their neighbour's cat, and Alex walked round to its home. The housekeeper came to the door.

"I thought I'd better bring him home as it's a bit wild outside, and he seems frightened by the noise."

"Not surprising. What a day! Never seen the like of it. I guess he escaped from the bucket this morning. Pretty little thing. Pity to drown 'em, but there you are."

"Drown them?"

"Yes. The gardener did it for Mrs Layfield this morning. I guess this one was too spry for him."

"I can keep him, then?"

"You're welcome, I'm sure."

Alex thanked her and returned to the house with the kitten, raging against the heartlessness of the world. If men ever had to answer for their treatment of the living creatures which shared their planet, there would be some bill to meet, she thought. She gave the kitten some warm milk, introduced it to Bella, who thought it a curious little object, and left them together while she went to telephone Ben to find out whether Nigel had changed his plans for collecting the books. She was afraid to try to contact Nigel himself at the Research Station for fear of interrupting him at an inconvenient moment, but she had to know what to do with the books before she left the next day. The telephone, however, was dead. The line had probably been blown down, she thought, as she went to the kitchen to make another pot of tea and eat the last of the cake.

When she returned to her room, the kitten slipped out, and Alex let him go, thinking that he could come to no harm in that empty house. After tea when she went to look for him, however, she could not find him. She searched the house from top to bottom. She went into Mrs Raynham's bedroom last, and saw that one of the long windows had been left open a few inches. As she went across to shut it, she heard the kitten's mew, and went out on to the verandah. This side of the house was sheltered from the wind, which seemed to be abating a little. The kitten mewed again, and looking up, Alex saw him perched precariously on the guttering of the roof, by the attic gable. He must have swarmed up the pyracantha that grew on the back wall of the house and from there had walked along the guttering. For one who had recently escaped being drowned, he showed singularly little respect for danger, she reflected, as she called to him enticingly. He arched his small back in response, but refused to budge, and began to mew again directly. Alex eyed the verandah and the expanse of pyracantha stretching to the roof. It was doubtful whether the shrub, tough and old as it was, would hold her, and it was a long drop down. She went to fetch a saucer of milk as bait, and balanced it on the verandah railing as she called again to the kitten, who responded with the same polite pleasure but budged not an inch.

"You went up, you can come down," said Alex, exasperated. It was getting dark, and she could not leave the kitten up there all night. It would freeze. The telephone was out of action, so it was no use appealing to the fire brigade. She tried for several minutes to entice the kitten down, but the vertical drop evidently had no appeal, and he kept up a constant complaint at his predicament.

In the end, Alex fetched an old shoe-bag from her room, slung it over her shoulder, changed her leather shoes for crêpe-soled canvas ones, and leaned over the boundary rail of the verandah. She tested the branches of the pyracantha. They seemed tough enough. It grew thickly, covering the brickwork, and somewhere beneath it lay the wooden trellis to which it had originally been trained. After a last unavailing appeal to the kitten, she climbed on to the verandah railing, tested the pyracantha again, and began to climb up it. The shrub had been trained round the verandah to meet again on the wall above the window, and Alex had decided to work back over the window before climbing vertically to the roof, since the fall to the verandah would be a comparatively short one, and she breathed a sigh of relief when she was no longer poised over the garden terrace. She hoisted herself on to the roof without much difficulty, but did not feel very happy when it came to working her way along to the kitten, who refused to leave the gable.

Standing on the guttering, splayed out against the slope of the roof tiles, Alex neither saw nor heard Nigel's footsteps below. He managed to stop himself from calling out when he caught sight of her, and stood there in an agony of helplessness while she edged her way along to the kitten. If he shouted, he would distract her, and it was too late to do anything but watch with a sick apprehension. Against the roof, that figure in navy slacks and a lemon-coloured sweater looked absurdly small. She was crazy to risk smashing herself up for a kitten, he thought angrily. At one point she stopped, as though dizzy, but she might have been waiting for a gust of wind to pass. Then she had the kitten by the scruff of the neck and had rammed it into the shoe-bag, jamming herself against the gable for support.

Alex, still unaware of his presence, tied the strings of the shoe-bag and slung it across her shoulder like a school satchel, ignoring the plunging of the small body inside. Edging her way back along the guttering, stopping once for the wind, she knelt cautiously when she was above the bedroom window, and lowered one navy-blue leg to grope for a foothold in the branches. Then she swarmed down the short distance separating the roof from the top of the window, working out a little to bring her down on to the verandah railing. Nigel held his breath as a branch broke away from the wall, but by then she had swung one leg on to the verandah railing and half jumped, half fell, safely inside it.

Angered by fear, Nigel called out as she stood up,

"Alex, are you crazy?"

And Alex, tired of the dismal day, of the gale, of empty dusty rooms, removal men and troublesome kittens, conscious of a grazed arm and trembling legs, snapped down,

"Yes. I am!" and disappeared through the bedroom windows.

He met her at the foot of the stairs and held her by the shoulders for a moment. She was still trembling.

"Sorry I shouted. You had me rattled. Are you all right?"

"Yes, thanks."

She released the kitten, which bounded away to the kitchen like a bouncing ball, and pushed her hair back from her forehead, leaving a dirty mark across it. Her hands were black, as was the front of her sweater, and there was a tear in one knee of her slacks.

"That was a very foolish thing to do, babe," he said gently.

"I couldn't leave the kitten there all night. He'd only escaped drowning by a hair's breadth this morning."

"So you risked breaking your neck or crippling yourself."

"It wasn't as risky as it looked. That old pyracantha is as tough as leather. Don't feel I'd want to be a tiler, though. I think I'll have a bath. The books are all ready in the study, Nigel. I thought you were coming earlier."

"I intended to, but couldn't get away. I tried to ring you about twelve, but the line was out of order."

"Well, help yourself," she said, and turned to go upstairs.

"When are you leaving, Alex? Can I drive you home?"

"I'm staying the night. The furniture which your mother didn't want in the flat is going to auction rooms, but it couldn't be collected until tomorrow morning, so your mother asked me to stay on and see it off."

"That's a bit bleak for you."

"Yes."

"Can I stay and keep you company this evening?"

"Do you want to?"

"I shouldn't ask otherwise."

"I'd be glad if you would," she said gravely.

"You look tired to death. Is there any food in the house?"

"Eggs. I was going to make do with those."

"Like to come out to dinner, or shall we share the eggs in the kitchen?"

"I think I'd better stay here in case your mother telephones. I expect they'll get the line in order again pretty quickly."

"Righto. Go and have your bath while I see what I can produce among the squalor."

She felt better after her bath, and raked out a dress from her suitcase, which was already packed, to grace the occasion. She found that Nigel had slipped out to the village and was unwrapping his spoils on the kitchen table: cold chicken and ham, tomatoes, crusty rolls, a piece of Stilton cheese, and a bottle of wine.

"Thought you might want the eggs for breakfast. By the look of it, you've existed on nothing more than cups of tea today," he observed, removing the unwashed tea-cups and the teapot to the draining board.

"I had an egg for lunch. It was difficult to get out with the men here. I promised I'd keep an eye on things."

"Just like my mother to leave you the dirty work. Well, as this seems to be the only table left in the house, we'd better make the best of it."

"My room's intact. We can go up there afterwards. That looks good, Nigel. I didn't think I was hungry, and now I find I'm starving. There's just enough cutlery here, I think, if we use the butter knife. The china's a bit rough, I'm afraid."

"But the company pleasant," he said gallantly, as he poured wine into two thick glass tumblers.

And suddenly the dreariness of the day departed, and that odd meal on the wooden kitchen table with an ill-assorted collection of cutlery and china suddenly took on a gay Bohemian quality which swept away the constraint Alex had felt with him.

They took their coffee up to her room. It was bare of most of her personal possessions, which had been sent off in her trunk the previous day, but it looked cosy compared with the stark emptiness of the rest of the house, and Nigel drew up his armchair to the electric fire and spread his long legs across the rug with a sigh of content.

"This isn't at all bad. Quite a snug little bed-sitter you've had here."

"Yes. My home for a year. It seems longer than that. So much seems to have happened."

"Has it been worth while?"

"Oh, yes. I feel I've learned a lot. There is no need to call me babe any longer," she said sternly.

He grinned as he took the coffee from her.

"I didn't think this afternoon's performance on the roof was particularly adult."

"I don't see what else I could have done."

"Borrowed a ladder, for one thing. The builders in the village could have obliged, I expect. Or that window-cleaner who lodges over the dairy."

"I was without transport and it would have taken me twenty minutes at least to walk to the village. Against that awful wind, too."

"It was easier to risk your neck."

"You don't stop to weigh up every little point. Anyway, it was easy," said Alex airily.

"Liar. Get over, Bella, you lazy lump. You're not the only one who likes the fire."

Bella, an inert mass in the middle of the rug, did not bother to uncurl as Nigel pushed her along a foot or two so that Alex could get her legs in front of the fire. The kitten, exhausted by the day's adventures, had eaten a large bowl of bread and milk and was curled up on the window seat, fast asleep.

"What's happening to Bella, by the way?" asked Nigel suddenly.

"She's coming home with me. Your mother was going to have her put down. That shook me."

"You've lost a good many illusions here, I guess. It was inevitable."

"Yes."

ALEX AND THE RAYNHAMS 173

"Well, it was time you grew up a bit."

"I was able to help, Beth, anyway. That's one item on the credit side. I went over to see them last week. They're so happy together."

"Match-making is a dangerous hobby, as Jane Austen pointed out in this," said Nigel, picking up a book from the lower deck of the coffee-table. "*Emma*. A very tiresome young woman, I remember."

"I wasn't match-making. Would you like some more coffee?"

"Yes, please."

"We'll want some more milk, then."

She disappeared with the milk jug, and Nigel returned *Emma* to its resting place and drew out Alex's field diary. It was kept meticulously, with all entries dated and many of them illustrated with small sketches. As she came in with the milk, a piece of paper slid out of the back of the diary. She snatched it off the floor and folded it quickly before putting it in her pocket. Nigel held out his hand.

"Please."

"Please what?" she asked blandly, as she poured the coffee.

"That letter. It was addressed to me."

"You are mistaken," said Alex firmly.

"My sight is pretty keen. Come on, my dear. Hand it over."

"No, I decided not to send it, as there was no point in it, and I'd forgotten it was there. I meant to tear it up. Forget it. Is that coffee too strong?"

"No. It's very good. I congratulate you on this diary. You're a good scientist."

"Thank you. Praise indeed."

She looked at him warily, and decided that he had accepted her ruling on the letter. She began to tell him about Peter's plans for his nurseries. When they had finished their coffee, however, Nigel removed the tray and asked her again for the letter.

"No, Nigel. I wrote it, and I have the right to withhold it. This is foolish. It's not of the slightest importance."

"Then there's no reason why I shouldn't read it."

"And no reason why you should give me orders."

"Do you give it to me or do I take it?"

He was standing now between her and the fire.

"What right have you to . . ."

She stopped as he caught her hands behind her and took the letter from the pocket of her dress. He looked surprised as he read it.

"So you brought the urns. Well, I'm blowed! I was wondering why the landscape gardener hadn't put them on his bill separately. I assumed he'd got hold of them, as he'd promised to keep his eyes open at a country house sale he was going to. They were just the answer. It was a kind thought of yours, Alex. Thank you. But why the reluctance to let me know that you were the kind donor?"

She looked down at her hands, wondering how to explain, wishing, not for the first time, that she was better at finesse.

"I thought . . . Well, it didn't seem worth calling your attention to it. We didn't want the urns at home."

"When did you bring them over?" he asked quietly, watching her through narrowed eyes. When she told him, he said, "That must have been quite a job. They're very heavy. You know, whenever you're trying to cover up, your voice is so casual that you give the game away immediately. It's so out of character. You give me a handsome present, you say nothing about it and you make an absurd fuss about my reading a perfectly simple, friendly letter. Come on, now. Let's have it."

"When you went away without saying goodbye, and didn't write, it seemed as though you'd had enough of me. Weren't interested. Then at Jane's you confirmed it. So the present seemed a bit like gate-crashing, and I decided that it was best left anonymous."

At this point, to her great relief, the telephone rang in the hall below and she ran downstairs to answer it. When she returned, Nigel was leaning back in the chair, eyes half closed, looking as though he was miles away in thought.

"It was your mother, to see if everything was all right. She'd been trying to get through ever since lunch-time."

Something in Nigel's look confused her, and she stopped to fondle Bella. The kitten woke, stretched, and yawned, showing a delightful little pink tongue, and then curled up into a ball and went to sleep again.

"What time are you leaving tomorrow?" asked Nigel.

"I'm not sure. I have to wait until the rest of the furniture has gone. The firm promised to be here at ten, so I hope to get away in the morning, but I've learned that it doesn't do to rely on promises of that kind."

"How are you going home? You'll be a bit loaded, won't you?"

"Yes. I thought, when I sent my trunk off, I could manage Bella and a suitcase, but now I've the kitten as well, I shall have my hands full. Clive would have come for me, but I couldn't give him any definite time. I'll manage, I expect."

"I'll come across in the morning and take you home. You can't mess about with trains and all that livestock."

"That's kind of you. Are you sure it won't be an awful bother for you?"

"My dear Alex, you've been an awful bother to me ever since you came here. A little more is neither here nor there."

"I thought so. That's why you cut it off so abruptly, isn't it? Because I was becoming a nuisance?"

"You read me like a book," he said mockingly.

"But, Nigel, friends needn't be a nuisance. Must you keep them out of your stronghold?"

"What are you pleading for, Alex?"

"Not to be completely shut out. I know you don't like getting involved with people, but I shan't be a nuisance in that way."

He chuckled and took out another cigarette, saying,

"This is fascinating. Do go on."

"Not if you're going to be objectionable."

"I'm not, truly. Just elucidate the words 'in that way'. I'm intrigued."

"I don't like you when you're being clever. You know

what I mean. I got over all that kind of foolishness with Bruce. I've finished with it, so you don't have to run away from me because I'm likely to become an embarrassment. Now what are you laughing at?"

"And you say you've grown up!" said Nigel, shaking his head. "My dear babe, you're talking out of your hat."

"Well, why, if it wasn't that, did you go without a word, and look at me as though I gave you a stomach-ache when you saw me at Jane's?" asked Alex furiously.

"I'm not admitting or denying the role you've given me; it's the one you've given yourself that's so absurd. Over with all that kind of foolishness, indeed. Be your age, girl."

With an enormous effort, she stifled her anger and made her voice light and casual as she said, with a shrug,

"Believe what you please. You certainly don't appeal to me in the way Bruce did, and I assure you that you are in no danger. I don't intend ever getting seriously involved with a man again. Bruce was enough. If, by any chance, it ever did happen, it would not be with you. Not my type. I just thought it would be pleasant to keep in touch now and again. We've found each other amusing, in short doses, I think. But please yourself, of course," she concluded airily.

"Quite a speech," said Nigel slowly, watching her through slits of eyes. "If I feel like an hour's amusement, I'll bear it in mind. Strictly platonic amusement, of course."

"Of course."

"What shall we play? Snakes and Ladders?"

"Oh, you're insufferable. So conceited and arrogant. You think that your charms are so great that every girl who knows you wants to invade that ivory tower of yours. I don't know why I bother with you at all. Go back to your comfortable, elegant home and keep the drawbridge up. I should hate anybody to disturb you, and chemicals must be so much more interesting than people."

"Sarcasm is not your strong point. You want to give it cold, not raging. You're being childish because you're over-tired. You've had an exhausting day. Go to bed and sleep on it. I'll be round in the morning."

"I am not in need of a Nanny, and you are certainly not suited to the part. Don't come round in the morning. I can manage quite well on my own."

"Do you mean that?"

She turned away from him, fighting the tears which threatened to overwhelm her. He was right. She was overtired with the strain of the past weeks, culminating in that stormy day, and she knew that she had behaved childishly. It was expecting too much of her tempestuous temperament, though, to ask her to admit it while her nerves were still taut and her body still aching with fatigue. It was a long time since she had been attacked by one of the childish outbursts of temper which had brought her so much trouble in her teens. Now it had to happen with a person whose opinion she valued more than anybody's, and one least likely to tolerate it. She knew that if she said that she meant it, he would go forthwith and not return in the morning. He always meant what he said, and asked the same honesty of others. He turned her round to face him, his face austere.

"Well?"

"No, I didn't mean it. Please go now, Nigel. I can't take any more today."

"Right. I'll be round at eleven. Good night."

He left her standing in the middle of the room, thinking miserably that if anything had been needed to confirm that his strategic withdrawal was justified, that evening had provided it. Emotional scenes with an irrational young woman were as out of place as a hair shirt in his comfortable, well-organised life. Tomorrow's goodbye would be final. She was sure of that. It was probably inevitable, anyway, but she went to bed angry with herself for mishandling the situation. She could at least have accepted the ending of their friendship with some restraint and dignity and not leave him with a last impression of childish tantrums and a feminine distortion of facts in a desperate attempt to keep the last link from being snapped. She knew him too well not to know what had brought that wintry look into his face.

The gale had abated, but it still moaned mournfully round

the house at intervals as she lay awake. Her last night in Pelham House. A fitting end to a year of disillusionment and blunders, she thought, sunk now in a determined pessimism. Bella was snoring, and she wished she had hardened her heart and bedded her down in the kitchen. The kitten had curled up with the dog, presumably unaffected by snoring. Alex burrowed down under the bedclothes to shut out the noise and despised herself for letting the tears have their way at last.

Chapter Twenty

AT eleven o'clock the following morning, Alex was sitting on her case in the front porch, with Bella lying at her feet and the kitten protesting loudly at the confines of the basket which imprisoned him. The house was empty, the keys deposited with the agent, and Alex, buttoning up her tweed coat and pulling on her gloves, was ready to be collected. All was to be cool and businesslike that morning, she had decided. No flap, no emotions. The gale had brought in its wake a day of gentle breeze and sunshine. She watched the play of shadows across the lawn as the birch trees swayed in a graceful mood after the torments of the previous day. Then the Jaguar came up the drive, and she stood up and grasped her suitcase.

"Good morning, Nigel," she said briskly as he stopped the car. "Don't bother to get out. I'm all ready."

"So I see. You looked very demure sitting there in the porch. Like Jane Eyre about to take up a new post. I'll give you a hand at stowing away the livestock. Where shall we put Bella?"

"She'll go on the floor in the back, I think."

They stowed the spaniel in without much trouble, for Bella now invariably stopped where she was put, and the cat's basket was jammed into a corner of the back seat by Alex's suitcase.

"Where would you like me? Shall I sit at the back and keep an eye on the animals?"

"They can't come to any harm." He opened the front door of the car and indicated the seat with an ironical little bow.

Before he started, she said in a matter-of-fact voice,

"About last night, Nigel. I'm sorry I made a fool of myself. Forget it, will you?"

"No. But don't worry about it now. I thought we'd go round the country way and keep off the main Elton Road. It's pretty congested with shoppers on Saturdays."

"Whichever suits you best. It's very kind of you to take me."

He shot a quick glance at her as he let in the clutch, but said nothing and they moved off down the drive, past the lodge, and away from Pelham House for ever. Apart from a few polite observations, the journey was a silent one. Nigel drove well, relaxed and cool, and there were no sudden stops and accelerations to make Alex wonder whether the kitten's basket was secure. Conscious that this was the last time that she would be with him, she found his presence both a joy and a sorrow.

Winter's bareness was everywhere around them, but in the flat stretch of country in the neighbourhood of Elton, the elms and oaks were silhouetted in a beauty of form that made them far lovelier than with their summer dress, and Alex wished she were an artist and could draw them. The clock in the High Street struck twelve as they emerged from a narrow, twisting lane into the town.

"I hope I'm not making you late for lunch," said Alex. "What time is Ben expecting you?"

"He's not. I gave him the day off to go to Twickenham. There's a good match there today and Ben's a rugger fan, as you know."

"Are you playing this season?"

"No. I've retired from the game. Too old."

"Where are you having lunch, then?"

"Oh, I'll probably get something in Elton after I've dropped you."

Alex was silent as she looked at her hands. A stilted formality now inhibited her. The silence became oppressive as the car swung along the lanes between Elton and her home. At last, on the home stretch, she said briskly,

"If you drop me at the end of the drive, Nigel, I can manage. Thank you very much. It was good of you to sacrifice a Saturday morning for me."

"We're devilish polite this morning," he observed with a little smile. "And very anxious to be rid of me. That's quite a long drive up to your house, I guess."

"I didn't want to bother you any longer than necessary."

"I told you last night about my attitude to the bother you've caused me. It still holds good. The few seconds I shall spend driving up to the house won't affect me, but will save you a long walk with some troublesome fellow travellers."

As they drew up outside Camerino, he said,

"What a lovely old place! You didn't overstate it, Alex."

"It is rather nice. Don't bother to get out, Nigel. I can collect the animals. Oh, there's Mummy."

Mrs Madison came from the house, smiling, followed by a slow-moving golden retriever.

"Hullo, darling. It's good to have you home again." She embraced Alex and turned to Nigel. "And you're Dr Lynton. How kind of you to bring Alex home! What have you got there, Alex?"

"A kitten. It would have been drowned if I hadn't adopted it. Do you suppose Bruno will mind?"

"Well, he's never liked cats, but I dare say he'll tolerate a kitten."

"Here is the second refugee," said Nigel, leading out Bella.

Alex was hugging the retriever, and Mrs Madison sighed and shook her head with a smile as her eyes met Nigel's.

"We're used to it, you know. The variety of lost or ailing

animals and birds that Alex has foisted on us during her lifetime would fill a zoo. Do come in, Dr Lynton. You'll be able to stay for lunch, won't you?"

"That's very kind of you. Thank you, I'd like to. Alex tried to throw me off at the end of the drive. I think she's had enough of me," he concluded with a bland smile for Alex.

"I'm . . . Funny," she said witheringly, and took Bella's collar.

"Shame on you, Alex. Come along in and meet some other members of the family, Dr Lynton. I assure you they're not all as graceless as Alex, and we shall be delighted to have you. My son and his wife are here today."

Chatting, they went in together, leaving Alex to introduce Bella and Bruno. What was he playing at, she wondered. He could be as smooth and unrevealing as a stone. All that charm would be laid on for her family, she didn't doubt, while her efforts to relieve him of her embarrassing presence were labelled graceless.

And so it proved to be. Nigel, at his best, made a most favourable impression, and he and Clive went off together after lunch to go over the estate. As Nigel had never displayed any great interest in timber, Alex suspected that this was a ploy, but to what end, she did not know. He had the kind of intelligent mind that was interested in delving down by-ways of new knowledge, however, and she might be maligning him in suspecting strategy. Perhaps all he had in mind was to pump Clive's brain, but he was foxy, and in his present mood, she didn't trust him. She consoled herself with a walk along the river with her sister-in-law.

"Lovely to have you as a person and not a mum," said Alex, as they set off.

"Good for me to get away from the children, too. We're lucky to have found such a good Nanny, though. I like the look of your friend, Alex. I was expecting to see a fair man, though. Did I have it wrong?"

"That was Bruce. He's married now. Nigel's the one who has just moved to a new house. The next thing is to start thinking about a new job, I suppose," she said, determined to keep the conversation off Nigel.

Sarah took the hint and they discussed jobs as they walked on, Bruno and Bella plodding along with them, two veterans who accepted each other with the toleration of old age.

Clive and Nigel were back before them, and were comfortably ensconced round the fire with the elders when they returned. Nigel, toasting crumpets and looking as though he'd been a member of the household for years, saluted her with his free hand and moved along the couch to make room for her.

"Just in time, girls," said Mrs Madison. "Charles, pass the plates."

Mr Madison put down his paper and did as he was asked. Passing one to his daughter, he said,

"Alex, do *you* know what's happened to those two urns we had in the rose garden? I've hunted high and low for them, but they've vanished."

"Of course I know. I found them thrown aside in the long grass last summer and I gave them to Nigel for his terrace. I told you at the time, Mummy."

"Did you, dear? I don't remember."

"Yes. The week-end of Elizabeth's first birthday. You must remember. I borrowed the car and took them there and then."

"Oh, yes, darling. It was those urns you were talking about, was it? I do remember vaguely."

"You were talking baby talk with Rosalind, and weren't paying much attention to me, but I definitely told you. Really, nobody in this house ever takes any notice of what I say. Pass the crumpets, Nigel, will you?"

"Well, I'm . . ." Mr Madison collected himself. "They were intended for the new pool we've been constructing in the front, but no matter."

"I insist on returning them," said Nigel, smooth as silk. "Alex left them as a surprise for me, and I didn't even know who had given them to me until yesterday."

"No, you keep them, my dear chap. Shouldn't dream of taking them back. Probably wrong for the pool, anyway."

"Of course they are," said Alex, wishing she had never seen the wretched things lying there on the grass. "In any case, two would be no use for a pool. You'd want four."

"Quite," said her father, adding a little plaintively, "All the same, Alex, you do have a habit of taking the law into your own hands, which can be awkward, to say the least."

"Treasured possessions vanish, lame dogs arrive," said Clive, grinning. "Never a dull moment with the youngest Madison."

"The urns shall be returned to their rightful home," said Nigel, accepting another crumpet from Mrs Madison.

"Certainly not . . ." began Mr Madison, when Alex interrupted violently,

"Oh, for heaven's sake! All this fuss about a couple of old urns. I'm sick of the things."

"It was a misunderstanding," broke in Mrs Madison. "They shouldn't have been thrown aside like that, Charles, if you wanted them. And I'm sure Nigel is very welcome to them. I don't fancy urns at the corners of the pool at all myself. I think it'll look like a tomb."

"That settles it, then, Nigel," said Mr Madison good-humouredly. "The urns are yours."

"I'm very grateful to you. I hope you'll come and see them some time and tell me whether you approve of their new site," said Nigel.

"Alex has a wonderful knack of putting her foot in it," said Clive mercilessly. "I just can't imagine her as a competent secretary. Didn't she bring havoc and confusion into your ranks?"

"My mother found her most efficient as a secretary. I didn't live in the house, so my opinion is only that of a bystander, but I felt a few ripples at the lodge."

"Havoc or not, we're all very glad to have her back," said Sarah.

"If I write a book about the river, Sarah, would you illustrate it?" asked Alex, determined to get this conversation away from the personal. Sarah welcomed this proposition with enthusiasm and a discussion on country books ensued.

After tea, Nigel, left alone for a few moments, strolled across the room and studied the portrait hanging over the fireplace. The old lady had a fine face, he thought. Strong, for a woman.

"Old Mrs Madison," said Sarah's soft voice behind him. "She died two years ago. A great loss to all of us. Greatest of all to Alex, I think. They were very close. And in character, very alike."

"There's a physical likeness, too," said Nigel slowly. "Not anything you can pick on, but it's there. The tilt of the head, and the mouth, perhaps."

"Yes. I notice it more in mannerisms, I think, and that fiery sparkle. Mrs Madison's hair is white there, but it was the same colour as Alex's when she was young."

Clive came in and joined them, putting a hand on his wife's shoulder as he said,

"A holy terror, was Grandma. I bet she led Grandfather a dance, poor man."

"I loved her," said Sarah gently. "She had such a warm heart under that formidable exterior."

Nigel liked this soft-voiced wife of Clive's. Although her pale, oval face had a dreamy quality, the dark-blue eyes were alive to the world. Good-looking, too, with that cloudy dark hair emphasising a creamy complexion.

"Alex is a chip of the old block," said Clive. "Strong-willed, impulsive and so obstinate sometimes that you could wring her neck, but somehow there's a warmth missing when she's not here. The old lady was like that. Living life to the full, with all her energy, right to the end. Tremendously involved in life. Far from peaceful to live with, but what a gap she left!"

"Personally, I'm all for a peaceful life," said Nigel, "but I know what you mean about the impact. Very distracting."

"That's an understatement. I'm with you about preferring a peaceful life. My wife is quite wonderful at creating it, too, in spite of the kids."

"Alex says I'm much too submissive. I've fallen off a lot in her eyes since our marriage, I fear," said Sarah, smiling.

"Alex says a lot of fat-headed things. No man wants to waste his energy on perpetual struggles when he's got work to do. If you value your peace, Nigel, you'll steer clear of the Grandma Madison strain. It takes too much energy to control," said Clive.

"You're right," said Nigel. "And now I mustn't trespass on your hospitality any longer."

"Come and see my workshops some time. I've some nice stuff there I think you'd like."

Nigel made a note of the telephone number and took his leave. Alex walked out to the car with him. It was dark and had turned cold, and he sent her back for a coat.

"Don't argue. I want a few words with you and I don't want you to catch pneumonia. Haven't had a chance to get you alone since we arrived."

When she came back, he took her arm and walked her a short way down the drive. It was very dark there, beneath the tall rhododendron bushes.

"Are you ready to admit that you were talking a lot of nonsense last night?"

She was silent and he took her in his arms and kissed her. He took a long time over it, and when he freed her, she rested her head against his shoulder.

"Will you admit it now?"

"Yes."

"That's better. Alex, do you know what I've always liked about you? What sets you apart in my estimation?"

"No. I can't imagine."

"Your blazing honesty. With yourself and others. You've never once put on an act with me, until last night."

"I know. That made you angry, didn't it?"

"Yes. Don't ever do it again. It's not necessary between us. You must know that."

"All right."

"You're darned bad at it, anyway. You'd never get away with it. Not with me."

"I know. That can be rather uncomfortable sometimes."

"You'll have to put up with it," he said, his free hand rubbing her head in a most comforting manner. "We can't stop here, or your family will send out a search party. Will you come over to lunch tomorrow?"

"I'd like to. I'd given up hope of ever seeing the inside of the house. Mother was quite right about those urns," she added, as they came to the pool in the centre of the lawn enclosed by the two wings of the house. "They would make it look like the family vault."

"They look very well on my terrace."

"Families are awful. They never realise when you've grown up. Especially if you're the youngest."

"Your family is rather nicer than most, I fancy. This has been a trying week-end for you, one way and another, hasn't it?"

"Yes. A proper mess. I don't know whether I'm coming or going. Isn't the moon fascinating when it's reflected in water?" she observed as they stood looking into the dark silkiness of the pool.

"Very. I'll see you tomorrow, then, and we'll see if we can sort things out a bit."

When Alex returned to the house, she wore an entranced look which was so foreign to her ebullient nature that it called forth a ribald comment from Clive, to which Alex responded with a calm smile and the information that she was tired out, and proposed to unpack her luggage and then go to bed.

"Well, what do you know?" asked Clive, as his sister left them.

"She looked almost peaceful," said Sarah, smiling.

"I liked that young man," said Mrs Madison, "but he wasn't what I expected. Didn't Alex mention that her friend was a fair person? When he was coming for the week-end, and then at the last moment, couldn't come, I distinctly remember some extravagant phrase about preparing for a young Apollo."

"That, dear, was a different young man," said Clive, grinning. "Our Alex seems to have been making good use of her time, I must say."

"What did you think of Nigel Lynton, Clive?" asked Sarah.

"Quite formidable, my dear. I didn't credit Alex with such good sense. Not that he gave anything away. Probably nothing in it, but he would be a match for the brat, I fancy, if he chose to embark on such an exhausting venture. What's your bet?"

"I think Dr Nigel Lynton knows exactly what he's doing," said Sarah, smiling, and refused to commit herself further.

* * *

"I moved from the lodge about three months too late," said Nigel. "I should have taken to my heels while you were engaged with Bruce."

Alex considered him over her coffee-cup. Sitting in the armchair opposite him, toasting her toes by the fire, she felt as complacent as a kitten after a saucer of cream.

"Should you?" she observed demurely.

"Yes. You have an insidious way of stealing up on one unawares. By the time I'd found refuge here, you were so entrenched that your ghost came with me."

"I wish I'd known. It would have consoled me. I was very unhappy when you left without saying goodbye."

"I know. It seemed the best way at the time. I've never wanted to hurt you, Alex."

"I know that."

"I told myself that it hadn't gone far enough to cause much damage. In my heart, I knew that wasn't true. Nobody could have given a clearer declaration of love than you over that silly business about Jane."

"I'm not very subtle, am I?"

"No."

"It wasn't meant to embarrass you. Only to stop you feeling so injured."

"Well, it certainly did that," he said, grinning. "It stopped me dead in my tracks. I'd armed myself against all feminine wiles, trained myself to watch for the subtle moves, and forgotten all about the strength of honest simplicity. I was far too clever. If you'd realised how strong it was, you would never have forsaken that suit on Friday night."

"I was tired and unhappy and desperate at the thought of losing you. A few crumbs would have done, I thought."

"They wouldn't, you know. We're in this thing too deep. And you, by nature, would never be content to do things by halves."

"What's your solution, then?"

"There's nothing for it but marriage," he said, holding out his hand. "Come over here and underline the consolations."

In his arms, reason gave way to emotion, and it was some time before words seemed necessary again.

"Dear Alex! I love you very much. I'll do my best to make you happy, but I don't feel I'm cut out to be the world's model husband. I'm serious," he said, as Alex nuzzled her head on his shoulder with a contented little sigh.

"I'm not worried."

"Well, you should be. I'm intolerant, fussy, devoted to my creature comforts, and absorbed in my job."

"I shan't start on a list of my failings; too morbid. I shan't expect to monopolise you, Nigel, if that's what you're afraid of. I shall have work of my own to do. Writing, I mean. I don't think I'm abnormally possessive. I've always appreciated freedom and independence too much. But it will be lovely to be together always, won't it?"

He looked down at the mobile, eager face which had haunted him so persistently over the past weeks. In the garden, he had remembered the look of tenderness and wonder in her face when she showed him a young bird or a toad or any living creature. In the house, he had been haunted by the integrity of those sea-green eyes, the warm vitality of her ardent spirit. And when he had seen her on the roof, fear had flayed his heart. There would be difficulties, he knew. He could not hope to preserve the smooth, even background of his life which left his energies intact for his work. Alex's impact was electric. She was impulsive, and strong-willed. Clive's warning had been a sound one. She would take a deal of handling, and his life would never be the same again. His quiet pasture, planned and guarded so ruthlessly for so many years, had been invaded by a force that would change the nature of every blade of grass. It was nature's own cunning which now made that old, peaceful pasture seem so dim and cold, and made him say with an odd little smile as he drew her closer,

"Yes, Alex, it will be lovely to be together always."

A MAGIC PLACE

Frances Barbury, her nerve shaken by her last theatrical venture, and envious of her elder sister's country contentment, becomes companion secretary to an invalid writer in his Welsh country home. His charming Dresden china wife and teenage daughter live with him. Frankie soon finds the peaceful atmosphere illusory. There is a mystery surrounding Trevor Falkland's literary silence and a scarce veiled enmity between his family and his pretty second wife Caroline. Stirring up troubled waters and seeking to create an open rift between Frances and Caroline comes Rolf, Trevor's son by his first marriage, a handsome, brooding, bitter and suspicious man, kind only to his ailing parent. Frankie treads warily between the opposing parties but finally must choose where her allegiance will lie.

THE TANGLED WOOD

Alison Blayde moves down to Sussex from London, jobless and romantically disillusioned. But when her Great-Uncle Arthur offers her the use of Corner Cottage for a minimal rent and financial backing to start a small library, it would seem that all her problems were solved.

Arthur departs the country with surprising speed, bequeathing to Alison his feud with occupants of Larchmere, the big house adjoining Corner Cottage. Yet the Ridgmont family edge themselves into Alison's life in such a way as to almost dispel the fears which had been haunting her since Arthur had left.

Nagging doubts disallow Alison to trust her neighbours and she is left swinging on a pendulum between doubt and confidence – and a long, long way from being out of the wood.

THERE IS NO GIFT LIKE THE PRESENT CORONET

IRIS BROMIGE
☐	15107 2	The Tangled Wood	20p
☐	16078 0	A Sheltering Tree	25p
☐	16077 2	Encounter at Alpenrose	25p
☐	17325 4	The Family Web	25p
☐	17843 4	A Magic Place	30p

RUBY M. AYRES
☐	12798 8	The Thousandth Man	20p
☐	14811 X	The Black Sheep	20p
☐	16173 6	Changing Pilots	30p
☐	17856 6	Wallflower	30p

HERMINA BLACK
☐	16079 9	Fortune's Daughter	25p
☐	17317 3	Theatre Sister At Riley's	25p
☐	17321 1	Who Is Lucinda?	25p
☐	17831 0	The House In Harley Street	30p

ELIZABETH CADELL
☐	15087 4	The Stratton Story	20p
☐	15088 2	The Past Tense of Love	20p
☐	16072 1	The Friendly Air	25p
☐	16073 X	Sugar Candy Cottage	25p
☐	17310 6	Home For The Wedding	30p
☐	17416 1	Honey For Tea	30p
☐	02791 6	The Lark Shall Sing	30p
☐	00335 9	The Blue Sky Of Spring	30p
☐	02794 0	Six Impossible Things	30p

All these books are available at your bookshop or newsagent, or can be ordered direct from the publisher. Just tick the titles you want and fill in the form below

---

CORONET BOOKS, P.O. Box 11, Falmouth, Cornwall.

Please send cheque or postal order. No currency, and allow the following for postage and packing:

1 book – 7p per copy, 2–4 books – 5p per copy, 5–8 books – 4p per copy, 9–15 books – 2½ per copy, 16–30 books – 2p per copy in U.K., 7p per copy overseas.

Name ....

Address ....

....